Playlist

This is the suggested playlist for Fallen. These songs have helped to set the mood and inspire me whilst writing this book.
Hope you enjoy them as much as I do!

Gone Too Soon – Simple Plan
Words That Don't Exist – Citizen Soldier
Trauma – NF
I Found – Amber Run
Lay By Me – Ruben
Die Too Young – The Band Perry
Dancing In The Sky – Sam Barber
Dangerous Hands – Austin Giorgio
...Fuck – Johnny Rain
Power Over Me – Dermott Kennedy
Version of Me – Sasha Alex Sloan
Twin Flame – Machine Gun Kelly
Never Stop (Wedding Version) – SafetySuit

Fallen

Lawson's Trilogy
Book 2

Elle Miller

Elle Miller
Copyright © 2024 Elle Miller
First Edition

The author has asserted their moral right under the Copyright, Designs and Patents Act, 1988, to be identified as the author of this work.

All rights reserved. No part of this publication may be reproduced, copied, stored in a retrieval system, or transmitted, in any form by or by any means, without the prior written consent of the copyright holder, nor be otherwise circulated in any form of binding or cover other than that in which it is published and without a similar condition being imposed on the subsequent purchaser.

This is a work of fiction. Names, characters, businesses, places, events and incidents are either the products of the authors imagination or used in a fictitious manner.
Any resemblance to actual persons, living or dead, or actual events is purely coincidental.

All available on Amazon Kindle Unlimited

Only suitable for 18+ due to nature of the book.

Trigger and Content Warnings.
This book contains the following adult themes and subjects:
Child Abuse / Death of a Family Member (Off Page) / Death and Murder / Graphic Depictions of Violence / Graphic Sex / Kidnapping and Abduction / Rape, Sexual Violence and Assault / Self-Harm and Suicide / Substance Abuse / Torture

Readers Notes

This book is the second in a trilogy and consists of three interconnected stand-alones.
They can be read as a series or separately, but I recommend reading in order.

Book I - *Vengeance*
Book II – *Fallen*
Book III – *Always* (*Coming Autumn 2024*)

*For everyone chasing their dreams... Keep going.
Run after them as fast as you can, and never look back.*

*To my readers – you made my dream possible.
I love you.*

Prologue

"Mi Vida, it's time to wake up." My sleepy eyes fluttered to the sound of my mum's voice. "We've got to leave for school in an hour." Already opening the blue star patterned curtains in my bedroom, inviting the rays of sunlight to spray across my bedroom, she glanced over her shoulder and offered me a soft smile.

"Good morning, mum. How are you feeling today?" This was a question I asked her every morning—and every night—as reassurance for myself before I left her to go to school, and a comfort before I went to sleep.

She's an addict—well, she *was* an addict. Until six months ago, when she got clean... again. This was by far the longest time she'd gone without sticking a needle somewhere into her skin though, and with every day she managed to make it through, the more I believed she would be alright.

She was getting back to her old self, back to the mum she was before my dad left us four years ago, when I was six.

Since then, it had just been us, and a few of her junkie friends adding to the mix along the way—or my *uncles* as my mum liked to refer to them as. They weren't my uncles; my mum didn't have any siblings, she was an only child—like me—and my dad only had two sisters, not that I'd ever met them before.

I think that's just what she called them to try and steer away from the fact they were the ones giving her drugs and making her sick. Maybe it helped with the underlying guilt she felt when she had a small child at home and was deciding to fill her veins with poison to chase a momentary high.

At the end of the day, I knew she had a choice, but they were the ones enabling my mum to ruin her life, marching her closer and closer to death.

"I'm fantastic darling boy." I believed her; she was beaming this morning, matching the sun that blazed through my window.

"Good, mum, I'm glad." It was the truth; I was happier about this more than anything in the world. She paused, analysing me as I sat myself up in bed, before taking her hand and moving my auburn hair across my forehead, leaning in closer to me and pulling me into one of her reassuring hugs.

"You're so grown-up Tanner, don't forget to be a kid, okay." She released me from her arms and placed a kiss on my forehead before turning on her feet towards my bedroom door.

When my dad upped and left, it hurt my mum, he didn't deserve her, and she didn't deserve to be treated the way that he treated her. Even though I was only little, the memories of how he acted towards her stayed with me. He was mean to her, and I think that if I hadn't been so young, he would have been mean to me as well.

Somehow, she managed to stay strong and appeared to

be doing okay, but then her parents were murdered in a home invasion, and that absolutely destroyed her, just like it did me.

I loved my Nanna and Pops so much, and I miss them every day, but I had to grow up quickly when my mum started using. I didn't have any other option but to. I was only young, and things started to go from bad to worse, she was losing control and I needed to step up and do what I could to be there for her. I learnt how to make myself ham sandwiches with the left-over dry bread, how to turn the shower on to the right temperature, and how to walk to school myself, all before the rest of the kids my age.

There was a day, about a year after my dad left; I was seven, she didn't turn up to collect me from school. She *always* picked me up—every day since I'd started—without fail.

I remember the worry flooding over me when the other students flooded through the gates of the school to head home with their parents. Everyone, except me.

I stood with my teacher, Ms. Marshall, and waited for what felt like a lifetime, with her arm draped around my little shoulders as the rain pelted down on us. She was the best teacher and she always made sure to look out for me.

"Tanner, I think we should take you to the office and wait for your mother there. I'm sure she'll be here soon, but we can't risk you catching pneumonia." She had said softly, ruffling my wild hair. "Come on, let's get you inside."

Forty-five minutes later, I was picked up by a man, he was smart looking; not suit smart, but you could tell that he looked after himself. His hair was perfectly combed over to one side with an excessive amount of hair product, and he sported a pair of Levi jeans and a Tommy Hilfiger bomber jacker. He'd told the lady in the reception that he was a family friend, and that my mum had come over unwell so had asked him to pick me up. He wasn't a family friend though, we didn't have any of those, and over time he'd turn out to be one of my *uncles*.

I'll never forget the conversation in the car, and when I say conversation I mean him speaking *at* me, telling me not to panic, he would look after me until my mum was better.

He didn't.

He was the first of many *uncles* to hurt me.

Pulling myself back to reality and out of the negative memories that rested inside of me, I sat myself up, threw back my bedsheets and twisted myself round, allowing my legs to dangle off the edge of the bed. I was tall for a ten-year-old; according to my mum, I got my height from my dad. I don't really remember much about him, and there weren't any photographs of him around the house, but she told me he was a lot taller than she was.

Stretching my arms above my head, I dropped them back down almost instantly in defeat as a sharp ripping pain shot through me. Closing my eyes, trying to steady myself from the sickening discomfort, I placed my feet into my perfectly positioned slippers that sat next to my bed.

This house was always cold, and even though the sun shone through my window, there always seemed to be a chill filling the rooms of the property. As the winter months settled in, it was almost unbearable to be here, but this was our home and there's nowhere else in the world I would rather be than here with my mum, even if I couldn't feel my toes sometimes.

Traipsing over to my mirror, I lifted up the top to my pyjamas, struggling as the cotton moulded against my skin. They were tight, but my mum couldn't afford new ones at the moment, so I settled for this pair, the biggest ones I had folded away in my drawer. Revealing an unhealed injury that had been formed on my skin by the last *uncle* that set foot in our home, I traced my small fingertip around the outside of the wound, flinching at the tenderness under my touch.

At least the others had healed okay, and my eyes didn't look black and blue like they had done a few months ago.

I don't know why, but this one wasn't getting better like the others. I'd taken care of it, just like I had with the other injuries before. In comparison, it was deeper—a lot deeper— and the chances of it scarring were definite. Every single other mark had left a permanent stain on my skin, so I knew that no matter how carefully I tended to this wound, I wouldn't be able to save my body from being tarnished with a scary reminder of how it got there.

JANUARY

Chapter One

TONIGHT, my mum, again, was nowhere to be seen. I'd hardly crossed paths with her for the last two weeks, and when I did, it was obvious that something wasn't right. She hadn't been herself. She was completely out of it and spent most of her time locked away, only coming out when this new man came round, which is when I'd scurry off to my room.

She was back to her old ways. I knew that she was using again. I knew the warning signs, I'd seen them a million times before. That's why he was always turning up. He was like all the others before, he wasn't nice, he did exactly what they used to do to me, worse than what they used to do to me.

As I sat in the lounge eating my bowl of dry cereal the door knocked, and out traipsed my mum from her bedroom. She looked withered, unkept and scrawny. I don't remember the last time I'd seen her eat, but it felt like a lifetime ago. I'd even started making her meals with the little food we had in the house and leaving it by her bedroom door, but everything I placed there was left untouched.

Making her way hastily toward the front door, I knew that was my cue to leave and stay out of their way. Shifting myself from the sofa I'd been settled on since I got home from school, I peered my head around my bedroom door to take a better look at the man she'd just let in. It was the same man. He was really tall—like abnormally tall—skinny, with a shaved head, and a scar above his left eye. Dressed in some tatty leggings and a beige jumper which took on hints of dirty grey, my mum stepped backwards, willingly allowing this man to cross the threshold into our house; a place that once again, no longer felt like home.

"You need to be quiet, Tanner's here." My mum droned out, she sounded high again.

"That little cunt's always here, I don't see how you've managed to keep him with you for so long. Look at the state of you." The man sneered, rolling his eyes at my mum.

"Don't call him that, he's my—" She stopped, her words trailing off into nothing as she caught me looking down the dimly lit hallway into the living room. The man's head turned, following the path of my mum's before turning back to her, not paying me any attention, staring straight through me like I was a ghost, acting as though I wasn't even there.

I slinked into my room, pushing the door closed. I knew why he was here, I knew he was selling my mum drugs, but there was nothing I could do to stop her, or him. I'd seen this too many times, her downfall was inevitable, and I don't know how many more attempts she would make and somehow pull herself from the hole before plummeting right back in there a few months later. All I could do was to stand by her and let her ride it out.

Although I was only a kid, I knew what she needed, and

I hoped that one day somewhere deep inside of her she'd believe that I was all she would ever need, that I would be enough. That she wouldn't have to fill this empty space in her life with the stuff that she so often put into her body. It was her escape from the harsh reality that she'd experienced over the last few years.

I slumped myself against the door and listened to the muffled words through the thin walls, only able to make out the odd word here and there. I listened so hard, that my head started to hurt, a swirling sensation hazing my view. I gave up and made my way to my bed, throwing myself down on the grubby covers. It didn't matter what was being said, she was going to take the drugs from this man, shoot up and get the high that she so desperately wanted.

I shut my eyes.

Chapter Two

WAKING to the sound of my door creaking open, I pulled myself up on my bed, a shimmer of light from the hallway creating a shadow in my room.

The man.

He pushed it open wide, and stayed positioned in the doorway, my squinting eyes trying to focus enough to make out the features on his face. I couldn't adjust them enough to focus clearly; the light that was now shining into them blew up his silhouette, casting the shadows of monsters across the walls.

"What do you want?" I spat at him on high alert. I wasn't scared, even if he was ten times the size of me.

"You know a mouth like yours will get you into trouble you little shit?"

"Fuck off." I gulped down, thinking that my mum would have clipped me around the ear if she'd heard me swearing at a visitor in our house, but I didn't care, he wasn't a visitor, he was a drug dealer and he was ruining mine and my mum's lives.

He was taking my mum away from me with these drugs he kept giving her.

He deserved it.

He was the devil.

Laughing at me as I attempted to warn him off, he snaked over to my bed, the smell of strong aftershave a sure reminder of what was going to happen. I held my ground, my eyes remaining pinned to where he stood.

I wasn't scared of him. I wasn't scared of anything anymore.

I knew that love was worth fighting for, and I only had to take one look at my mum, and I was ready to go to battle. I would try to do what I could to protect her, even if it resulted in me getting hurt. At the end of the day, that's what war was, right? The noble willingness to put yourself through suffering in order to keep the people you care about safe.

What was he going to do, push me around? Put cigarettes out on my skin? It didn't bother me like it used to. I'd had that done so many times before that I'd almost become desensitised to the feeling.

"You're going to kill her; you know that right?" I glared over to where he was standing, wishing for him to disappear.

"I don't care what happens to her." His words cut me deep. How can one human being not care about another. My mind raced, trying to find some smart-ass come back, but I drew a blank.

I continued to stare at him.

"Look, she makes her own decisions. If she wants to fuck me for drugs, then I'm not going to say no." He taunted, riling me up even more than I already was. "She's a druggy whore, and I'm not going to say no to sticking my dick in something." The way he spoke about my mum was enough to push me over the edge. I saw red, and nothing in this world could stop me as I lunged my small body towards him, balling my fists I shot the first blow to somewhere just above his waist. I hit out again, and again and again. He didn't move, I knew he wouldn't, he was huge, and I was a tiny dot in comparison.

Grabbing my wrists, he held them tightly to stop me from lashing out more than I already had and slammed me into my chest of drawers next to the door.

"I hate you!" I screamed, hoping my mum would hear me and save me, but she didn't.

"Listen up, you little cunt. You have no idea who you're messing with here." He said between gritted teeth, and I tried to break free from his grip. I tried so hard, throwing myself around hoping to loosen him from around me. Bringing my arms down in front of my face I strained my neck forward and bit into his hand, hard enough to pierce the skin.

"You fucking shit." He bellowed as he took hold of my hair with his uninjured hand and violently smashed my head into the wall. Undoing his belt, he freed it from around his waist and wrapped it around his knuckles, leaving half of it hanging free. I knew what was about to happen, I might only be ten, but I wasn't dumb.

Lifting it back above his head he cracked it down across my back, the sting radiating through my skin.

Another strike.

And another.

And another.

Until I couldn't take anymore.

I fell to the floor, my knees giving out underneath me. Using the little strength I had in my arms, I tried to pull myself towards the door of my room and towards the light that seeped through the gap in the door from the hallway.

Whipping the belt down again, it smacked against the back of my legs which had now become bare, my pyjama bottoms now rolled down as I tried to drag myself along the hard wood floor towards my bedroom door, the pain even harsher on my naked skin compared to through my clothes.

Tears streamed down my face, but I knew that I had to at least try to get through the agony and away from him. He stopped and stood there, watching over me, my dignity and strength to fight now strewn across the floor along with my pyjamas.

"You'll regret ever doing that. I'm going to make you pay." My room now felt colder than it ever had. I was numb, yet I could feel the pain of every single mark that he'd made on my body, the blood dripping down from my forehead, the bruises forming on my back and legs from the whipping he'd just given me. Just as I managed to reach the door, he pulled me back into the room and threw me across the room with ease, like he had some kind of super-villain strength.

"M-mummy, mummy..." I whimpered, using the last of my energy to call out for someone who was meant to protect me. I knew she wouldn't come, but I called out for her anyway.

"She's not going to save you. No one ever will. You're on your own. Look at you." His laugh cooled my blood, his sinister mocking making me realise that he was right.

No one would ever save me.

Somehow, I managed to tug myself up, leaning my back against my bed, wincing at the frame pressing into my battered skin. The man turned, planting his two feet directly in front of me, and towered over my body as I curled myself into a ball in a final bid to protect myself. I focused on his white trainers which were now artistically splattered with my blood. I could feel his eyes piercing into the back of my head, but I didn't break away from his shoes, or the traces of my blood painted upon them. I had tried to stay strong for so long, yet the tears continued to fall from my eyes landing in a puddle of shattered hope on the floor.

It was in that moment that I knew that I didn't need to try to be stronger, I just needed to be safe, something that over the years, I'd become so unacquainted to. My mum had broken my heart over and over, time and time again, but somehow, I still managed to love her, even with the tiny fragments scattered across the corners of our home.

"Look at what you did to my trainers." He grimaced. I didn't look up, instead I remained locked onto his feet and tried to zone out from his words and the pain scorching my skin.

I'd never felt scared, but at this point in time, I didn't know how I was going to make it through this, I had no idea whether I would make it out alive.

His trainer connected with my face.

Darkness.

Chapter Three

OPENING MY EYES, my vision was blurry, and my head felt heavy. The hallway light still flooded into my bedroom, and I lay there, motionless on the cold floor. As I came round, I remained silent, focusing on the rhythm of my heart as a reassurance that I was still alive.

Remembering the beating that I'd taken from the man, if he was still here, I knew that if I moved or made a sound, the chances were that I'd get another strike or two with the belt. I listened out for some indication that he was in the house.

Silence.

Not a sound.

With my body curled up on my bedroom floor, I allowed myself to quietly cry, my entire body trembled in unison with my sobs. I'd experienced abuse at the hands of these men, but this was by far the worst time it had happened. Normally it was a cigarette burn or a quick backhand around the back of the head, almost done to mock me because I was just a defenceless child, but not since the first time had I cried out for my mum; not once had I been left for dead in the house that was meant to be my safe place.

The first time one of these men laid their hands on me, it was the man that picked me up from school. After the drive home, where he somewhat convinced me that he would stick around and look after my mum until she got better, my life took a painful and horrifying turn.

That afternoon when I got home, as I made my way through the front door to our house, I looked through into my mum's bedroom, only to see her sprawled across her bed through a crack in the door. I remember thinking that she was dead until she started coughing and spluttering and gasping for air, as though something had ripped her soul from her body.

At the time I didn't understand what was going on or why she was in the state she was, all I knew was that the man who picked me up from school had promised to take care of her. She lay there, trying to inhale whatever air she could.

"Move." The man demanded, treating me as if I were a dog. I remained in the spot my feet had frozen me to, not moving one single inch, just staring wide-eyed at my mum.

"I said move."

I didn't.

The smell of cigarettes filled my lungs, as a plume of smoke brushed past my face, and that's when it happened. That was the moment that I got my first scar from these monsters.

He burnt me. He burnt me really bad.

The first of my mutilations was placed to the side of my neck. Although it had gradually faded over time it still remains noticeable even now, but the memory of it happening is the worst. I will keep it in my head for as long as I live, and I know it will remain there, no matter how hard to try to free it from my mind.

That was the first time I called for my mum whilst being abused at the hands of these men.

STILL ROLLED UP IN A BALL, I slowly started to try and calm myself, as hard as it was, I realised that I needed to somehow get up and make sure my mum was okay. I ached from head to toe, but I managed to find the strength to pull myself up onto my bed, flinching as the pain stormed viciously through my frail body.

I was still naked from the waist down and my legs were tarnished with bloody gashes that matched the ones I could feel strewn across my back. My brain shook violently in my head as blood started to run down my face; bringing my hand up to my eye, I felt along the split in my skin just above my eyebrow.

Dark crimson covered my tiny fingers, but this wasn't the first time I'd seen my own blood due to the work of someone evil, and I never expected it to be the last, no matter how many times I had wished it was.

Looking down at my hands trembling in my lap, I also noticed my top that had been shredded along with my skin, bloody and ripped. I stared at my palms for the longest time, trying to make sense of what had happened and what might happen next.

I knew that I shouldn't have talked back, the man was right, my mouth would get me into trouble. He proved that to me. But I couldn't take anymore, for years I'd been left to these random men. Left by my own mother, and all for what? For drugs, for my mum's addiction, for them to get their own sick and twisted kicks out of.

My life hadn't been fair to me, in fact I'd been through enough to last someone a lifetime, yet I still managed to fight. Truth be told, I was growing tired. I was *ten* and I was tired of this thing called life. This wasn't a life and part of me had wished that this last man had killed me. I couldn't face going through this again, I couldn't bear the thought of being forced to stay in my room whilst some creep used and abused my mum.

The only thing that kept me here was my mum.

Sliding myself off of my bed in pain, I bent over to retrieve my pyjama bottoms from the floor, the hurt in my stomach unbearable as I attempted to pull them on over my injured legs.

Holding back the tears forming in my eyes, I steadied myself on the wall and made my way to the door. As I got to the entrance I paused, remaining cautious and fully aware that he potentially could still be out there. I stayed there hunched over for what felt like an eternity before deciding to peer around the door and venture out into the hallway.

With the floorboards creaking beneath my feet, I left a trail of blood as I dragged myself along the corridor towards my mum's room. I never knew what state I would find her in, sometimes she would have already come round from her drug induced coma and would be dealing with the aftereffects, other times she'd be laying there breathing so slowly that on occasion I thought she'd died.

As I reached her room, the door was still pulled almost closed, but the light was now off, making it impossible for me to see anything inside. I gulped down my anxiety like I always did before pushing through the chipped wooden door.

Letting the light from the hall rush into the room I could make out my mum still laying on her bed and although my memory was a bit hazy from having taken a beating, it appeared that she was still in the same clothes as she'd been in for the last couple of days—the standard funeral black jumper dress. I stepped into the dimly lit area and crept over to the lamp which was positioned on her bedside table.

Twisting my body away from where she was resting, I tried to compose myself and hide the pain I was in just in case she came to.

She didn't.

Instead, she just lay there.

Unnervingly motionless.

Sidestepping, the light from the bedside table lamp doused her body, and with my eyes trying hard to focus I stood there as shockwaves of alarm shot through me. Inspecting her from the other side of the bed, I could see a needle embedded into her neck. I'd seen many needles hanging out of my mum's body before, but not there.

Pressing my two fingers into the other side of her neck, I felt for a pulse; something that I'd had to do a handful of times before. Unlike those occasions, there wasn't a pulse, there was no reassurance that she was still alive. Instead, I was met with nothing but her icy skin.

I sagged down onto the floor and took her hand in mine, her skin cold to the touch, and I sat there holding onto the one thing I had left in this life.

Someone who had been the makeup of my past and my present.

Someone who was no longer my future.

I sat and held onto *her*.

I didn't know what else I could do but wish for her back.

I felt like I'd spent the last few years stuck in this hell that I called my life, hoping that one day I would escape it with my mum by my side. I focused on how our future would be so amazing, so beautiful, just her and I. It was something I used most days to escape the cruel and sad reality that was my life.

Drowning in a tidal wave of war and grief, of the consciousness that I was now all alone in the world. All the love that I wanted to give my mum had nowhere to go now, my heart was completely hollow. There was so much I wish I could have done to protect her from them, to help her when she couldn't help herself.

Climbing onto the bed next to her, I suddenly felt myself becoming weak and tired, the universe had bled me of everything that I had to live for, and I didn't know how to, or whether I even could come back from this.

I lay there next to her, one hand covering my mouth as I choked back the sound of my sobs, my other hand cradled my chest, trying to subside the mutilating pain in my heart whilst tears ran down my cheeks and onto the pillow.

There would be no happiness after her.

Chapter Four

THESE STREETS WERE scarier when it was dark, but nowhere near as frightening as the thoughts racing through my head. Shadows on the walls and the beeping of traffic filled me with dread. I wiped my eyes, hoping that the constant stream of tears would finally stop, just like I hoped the scars that were scattered across my body would disappear.

But they never did. They remained on my skin, a constant reminder of how I got them, of the pain, of the suffering. I didn't understand how anybody could happily provide someone the means to potentially kill themselves, or how these men could inflict the pain they had on my small body. They treated me like I was an animal, caged in a world full of suffering with no way of escape.

I was only a kid. A small, defenceless kid.

I walked, and walked and walked around the city of London, with no idea where to go, or what I would do when I got there. All I knew was that I had to get away. Away from that house, away from her lifeless body, away from all the places that reminded me of her.

Walking past the playground that we'd spent the summer holidays in last year, I batted away the tears that streamed down my face, my heart sinking at unexplainable rates. I would never get to make more memories like that with her. I would never get to lay on the grass and look up at the clouds and laugh with her about what kind of animals we could see in them. I would never experience the summer sun on my skin with her next to me. I wouldn't be able to roll my eyes at her when she tried to put a silly sun hat on my head like I was a baby.

No more hugs. No more conversations.
No more of her smell. No more of her voice.
No more of any of her.

Making my way through Highpoint Park, I somehow managed to carry on putting one foot in front of the other until it became almost impossible for me to travel any further. The frosty winds made it hard to focus on anything except how cold my battered body was.

It must have been nearing minus temperatures outside, and as I walked coatless and shoeless, I started to give up the fight, my legs beginning to give way. My body seemed to be going into a state of shock and mentally, my ability to continue along these streets decreased, along with my willingness to stay alive.

Finding a bench, I pulled myself up onto it and curled myself into a ball, doing everything I could to try and warm myself up. Wrapping my frail arms around myself, shivering as if someone had dumped me in the middle of Antarctica without a single piece of fabric upon my skin. I lay there, alone, quiet, and utterly defeated by the hand that life had dealt me.

It's okay, just close your eyes.

You don't have to fight anymore.
Just give up and be with her.

Chapter Five

"Son, are you okay?" An unfamiliar voice whispered softly into my ears. "Can you hear me lad... Jesus, Dax, give me your coat... Quickly... That's it, you're okay now..."

Shaking uncontrollably as I was hoisted up into the arms of a stranger, I managed to muster up the energy to try and free myself, scared that one of the men from my past recognised me and was about to take me away and inflict more pain on my body.

"No, no, no!" I battled against the person who was now holding me close against his chest. "Please don't hurt me," I whimpered, my voice cracking as I strained out the four words that no kid should have to say with genuine concern for their life.

"It's alright kid, *you're* alright, I've got you." The stranger reassured in a tone so authentic, that I almost believed that for once, I might *actually* be okay. The heat of his body radiated through me as I nestled my face into the wool of the scarf wrapped around his neck.

With every step he took, I gradually started to come round from the blackout I'd been in since God knows when.

I had no idea where he was taking me, but it couldn't have been any worse than where I'd come from.

The sound of a car door opened near to where we were; if my head wasn't feeling so heavy, and I hadn't had been so obsessed with the heat and respite this strange person was offering me, I would have looked up. I didn't care where we were, or where we were going, all I knew was that I needed this feeling of safety that was washing over me. As alien as it was, I welcomed it.

"We need to take this lad to the hospital, Hank." The man said, bundling me into the warmth of the vehicle, and before the car door had even closed, we were off.

"It's okay son, you're safe now... What the hell were you doing out there..."

"Dad, is he okay? He doesn't look so good... He's so white... What's wrong with him?"

"Dax, don't worry, we're going to take care of him."

I phased in and out of consciousness for the duration of the journey, completely unaware of where I was, who I was with, or where we were going. All I kept focus on was how my body slowly stopped trembling, and how the hands of this person, which were tightly wrapped around my back and head, gave me a somewhat slither of faith that I might be safe from all of the monsters in this world.

I hoped to hell that I was.

"Mr. Lawson." I blinked my eyes open, the brightness of the lights above me made my head throb along with the rest of my body which had slowly started to give up on me. A stifled groan escaped me, alerting them that I was conscious.

I could feel the eyes of everyone in the room turn; their attention now directed at me.

"Hey there lad, you gave us quite a scare." I tried opening my eyes again but failed miserably. The florescent lights were blinding and no matter how hard I tried, I couldn't keep them open.

I wished someone would turn off these lights.

Grimacing as pain crashed through my body like flooding rivers breaking down the dams of a city, a gentle hand placed itself on my shoulder and my heart warmed slightly.

"You need to rest little buddy." A different, but still just as concerned, voice struck my ears, this time it was a little closer. "Can someone switch those goddamn lights off!" Within seconds the room that was so brightly lit fell into a softer glow.

"It's okay mate, we'll look after you." Another alien voice.

How many people were in this room?

Why were they all so caring?

Was I dead?

"W-where am I?" I choked out, my eyes now semi-open, starting to focus on the room and people surrounding me. "Y-You need to go back and get my mum." I could feel the tears starting to build as the harsh reality of my mum's death hit me again like a tonne of bricks to the back of the head. It wasn't a nightmare; she really was gone. I tightly closed my eyes, wishing that when they opened again, I would be back with her in our little apartment, watering the flower box outside of the kitchen window.

Silence filled the room around me, and I begged for someone to say something, I needed to hear something, anything other than the humming and signals of the hospital equipment that reminded me that I was still alive on this planet.

Without her.

Moments went by and no one said a damn thing, instead they just looked at one another as though I was crazy. Maybe I was going crazy, maybe I'd just bumped my head, and this was all a dream, maybe I was going to wake up in a second and all of this would have just been a terrible, terrible nightmare.

I never wanted to wake up for school, but I would use all of the wishes in the world to have my mum standing by my window opening the curtains, still clean from drugs, and I'd silently curse her for making me get up.

Squinting my eyes closed tight, I prayed that when I opened them again, I wouldn't be here, I prayed that I'd be in my own bed, away from these strangers and back with her.

"Shh, it's okay," a gentle hand brushed itself across my forehead.

"No, no, no!" I struggled to break out of the wires connecting me to bleeping hospital machines around my bed, I needed to get out of here. "S-S-She's... dead." I managed to spit out, my voice quivering, as I collapsed back into the mattress of the hospital bed in defeat, my eyes blinking to the sounds of the monitors.

"What's your name lad?" The older man's voice shattered the painful silence, asking a question I knew the answer to.

"My name is Tanner Campbell, I am ten years old and I live down Magnolia Terrace, in a flat above Mr. Baxter's butcher shop." I mumbled out robotically, speaking the exact words my mum had drilled into me, the information I needed to give to someone if I ever got separated from her.

"I need to go back there, p-please, you don't understand, I need to go and get my mum." I flicked my eyes between the nurse and the strangers surrounding my bed.

Moving his eyes away from me, he focused on another older man who was stood at the entrance to my hospital room. "Hank, can you make your way round there please? Call the police on the way there, let them know we have Tanner Campbell here." He stepped away from my bed and towards the other adult male. "Let me know what you find."

Walking out of the door, this Hank guy gave a clipped nod of his head.

"Will do Garrett." Then he left.

"Tanner, we will find her, but you need to sleep, you need to get better. Can you do that for me son?" He asked, a question so simple, it was only sleep, I could easily do that, but whenever I shut my eyes, all I could see was her, laying there without me.

I'd left her.

I couldn't say anything, for the longest time I just stared at the wall in front of me, and in a joined commitment, they all pulled up chairs and sat around my bed, until my eyes grew heavy, and I surrendered to the exhaustion from the events of the last twenty-four hours.

APRIL

Chapter Six

I SAT LOOKING out onto one of the many gardens of the grounds out of the window in the office – a place I'd recently found that helped to put a slight cease-fire on my emotions, the rays of sun started to fade out in the horizon.

Death had grabbed her by the hand and taken her away from me, leaving me alone and lost in this big world. I didn't know how much loss a kid could carry on their shoulders, but mine was excessive.

The last three months had made me realise that the world would undoubtedly carry on turning whether my mum was here or not, all I knew was that things would never be the same. She was gone and I would carry on searching for her in every sunrise and sunset, even though I knew full well that I would never see her again.

It turns out, the only next of kin I had on my hospital records was dead, I didn't have anyone else, no one. Just my mum.

My dead mum.

Since leaving the hospital after being treated for

hypothermia, I'd been put into foster care with the people that saved me on that cold January morning. The ones who refused to leave my side, even during out of hours, they had stayed right next to me. Turns out they thought I'd be better off being with them rather than in the care system.

They'd taken me in as though I was their own son and brother, they had brought me into their world without any hesitation to include me in their lives. Garrett Lawson was the father of Dax and Kian Lawson, I don't know what he did for work, but it must be a hell of a good job, because their house was *massive*. A big country manor, with acres of garden, enough to fit a thousand football pitches in.

The ceiling to the foyer reached the entire height of the house, and I wondered how anyone managed to get up there to clean it. The neutral tones swept through the property and although there wasn't so much as a bright colour in sight, the house felt homely and welcoming, which made it slightly easier to live in considering all I wanted to do was be back with my mum in our run-down place.

My bedroom was bigger than the apartment that me and mum shared. There was so much space in just this room alone, and sometimes it was daunting. I'd shut myself away in the walk-in wardrobe, just to feel a sense of calm, the endless amount of space felt too much for me some days. The king-sized bed that was made up for me to sleep in swallowed up my body, and in all honestly, even though I was safer here than I ever was with my mum, I couldn't help but feel scared.

I needed to feel small.
I needed to feel her.

For the first few weeks of being here, I didn't speak, I hardly ate, I couldn't navigate through things without breaking down, I was lost without her. But the Lawson's never gave up on me, not once did they get frustrated that I wasn't speaking, or mad at me when I flipped out, or offended at the fact I'd appeared to have left my manners back at Magnolia Terrace.

They didn't abandon me, no matter how hard it got for me to cope some days. Through thick and thin, through my pain, tears, and anger at how cruel life had been to me, they stuck by my side. Garrett had even organised and paid for a funeral for my mum, it wasn't big, my mum had left her friends in the past, and when she started using they had all dispersed into thin air. I guess no one wanted to be associated with the drug addict mum from Magnolia Terrace. There was only me, Garrett, his two sons and Hank – Garrett's best friend, the driver. They were all there.

I couldn't fathom out why they'd accepted me—all of me—all of my trauma, my hurt, my hatred towards the world, but for some reason they had, and I know that most of the time, I hadn't shown how grateful I truly was for them all.

They had given me a place in not only their home, but in their lives as well. They included me in every single part of their day, from eating with them when I felt like it, to being invited out into the gardens to play football with Dax and Kian. Movie nights in and days out, I was there for all of it, I was never excluded, which I guess throughout my life is something I'd become accustomed to.

Ultimately, my mother's heart had remained faithful to drugs, more than her drive to stay sober for me. Forgotten about and left to fend for myself, it had become apparent that after her death I'd been walking around with a burning pit of angst and loneliness in my stomach for God knows how long.

Maybe I'd swallowed it down in the hope that she would actually be able to stay clean and we could live a life I had only ever dreamed about. Her death just magnified the resentment I felt about the situation I was in, as well as towards her.

The sun had completely set, I don't know how long I'd been sitting here for—time seemed to be merging—about an hour or two perhaps. I hadn't seen or heard from Garrett, Dax, or Kian for a while though. Usually, they'd pop their heads in to check in on me, even if they didn't say anything, I could sense their presence standing in the doorway. The feeling of someone checking in was nice, it meant they actually gave a damn about me.

Shutting my eyes and taking a deep breath in, filling my lungs with the newfound life I had discovered by being here, I dangled my legs off of the windowsill I'd been perched on and paused there staring down at the perfectly positioned rug on the floor. Another one of my internal battles ignited, one where a simple spark could set me off; those ones were the conflicts where I was trying to remember everything about my mum but let her go at the same time, and those were the hardest to deal with.

She had always been a star in my eyes, but I guessed now, she was just a more distant one than she was before, and I needed to come to terms with the fact that she really wasn't coming back, even though it killed me to admit that.

Dropping my feet down to the floor, I dragged them across the mahogany boards of the office, tiptoeing into each plank and carefully avoiding the joins in the wood as I made my way over to the doorway. The room was dark now, only lit by the lights which had been switched on in one of the many hallways of this mansion.

"Hey Kiddo." I was met by Dax, the eldest of Garrett's sons. He was ten years older than me, making him twenty; he was super cool, I liked him a lot. Ruffling my hair, he picked me up and placed me on his hip with ease. He was tall and strong, everything that I wanted to grow up to be.

"Where have you been little man? I've missed my partner in crime today." I felt his lopsided smile against my cheek as I nuzzled further into his neck. Since being here, the only place I'd truly felt safe had been in this person's arms. Don't get me wrong, I was so grateful for Garrett and Kian, but there was something about Dax that made me feel as though he would never let harm come to me as long as he was walking this earth. He'd become like a big brother to me in such a short amount of time, he'd even let me sleep in his bed with him when I got sad at night and the tears became too much for me to deal with in my bed alone in the dark.

"I've been around, the question is, where have *you* been?" I grinned back at him, gums and teeth showing.

"Woah, I can see that my backchat is clearly rubbing off on you!" He laughed, making his way down the long corridor towards the staircase, but before we made the descent, he placed me back down onto the floor and lowered himself onto his knees so he was level with me.

"It won't always feel like this, Tanner, okay." Placing his arms on my shoulders, I could see a type of sadness in his eyes, the same type I saw when I looked at my reflection in the mirror. "You know, I lost my mum when I was thirteen, so I know what you're going through." Running his hand through his hair, he pulled me into one of his bear hugs that I'd grown to love since being here. "Just remember, that we're here for you." His words in that moment meant everything to me, and it all started to make sense as to why they'd accepted me so easily into their lives, maybe because Garrett and his sons knew exactly what was going on inside this little brain of mine.

"Can you do something for me though, Tanner?" He released me, after squeezing me so tight that I thought I might explode. Nodding in apprehension my stomach knotted as I wondered what he could want from me.

"Promise me, that no matter how bad those thoughts in your head get, you will always talk to me. Don't keep things bottled in." The tone of his voice had altered, almost shattering under his own words, defeated at the possibility that this was a piece of advice he wished he'd been given when his own mum had passed away.

His blue eyes kept focused on mine as he waited for me to answer. I didn't know if that was something I'd be able to do, but what he'd just said to me spoke volumes.

"I'll try my bestest, Dax." And I would. He made me feel like I could speak to him about anything.

"Good lad, now let's go get something to eat."

"Why are we having pussy for dinner?" Dax stepped back and let out the most wholesome sound I'd ever heard.

"Where the hell did you hear that?" He responded between his fits of laughter. I raised an eyebrow. I didn't get what was so funny.

"I heard you speaking to someone earlier, and you said something about eating pussy. I thought you might have been on the phone to the butchers and that's what we were having for dinner. I don't really want to eat a poor cat though, you know, I think I'd rather have chicken instead."

"Oh Tanner." His laugh echoed through the hallway. "We'll make a Lawson of you yet kiddo. Come on, let's go get some *real* food." He picked me back up and threw me into a piggyback and ran down the stairs, turning towards the kitchen as we got to the foyer.

Popping me down onto my feet before we entered the kitchen, Dax looked down at me and winked.

"Let's not mention about eating any cats to dad, yeah."

"Gotcha."

Chapter Seven

"TANNER!" I jumped out of my skin and abruptly out of the deep sleep I'd managed to fall into, startled by Kian's voice.

"W-What's wrong? Is everything okay?" I questioned, my body on edge, never knowing when the next bad thing was going to happen to me. I had a feeling that I would always worry about when something bad was going to happen, because let's face it, I didn't know any different.

"Dude, why are you in the wardrobe, *again*?" Kian shook his head and grinned at me. I knew he thought I was weird sleeping in here, but it was the only place I managed to feel safe enough to get some real rest. I wasn't exposed like I was when I tried to sleep in the bed out in the big room.

He reached for my hand that I'd already offered up to him. Kian was less athletic than Dax, shorter too, but with the same blue eyes that each member of the Lawson's had. Although each of the brothers looked like Garrett, they didn't look overly similar to one another, except for their eyes. He was shorter than his older brother, and his temperament was considerably different. They both boxed, but where I saw Dax doing it for fitness, something told me that Kian did it so he knew how to fight, that maybe, he *wanted* to fight. I'd seen his angry a couple of times, not at me, nor at Dax or Garrett. It was usually someone at school that had wound him up, and I knew he'd been suspended from Oakland a couple of times for fighting.

Something made me consider that maybe the loss of their mum had affected them both in different ways. Whilst Dax seemed to be self-aware about his actions and people's feelings, it was the complete opposite for Kian, and it made me question where I would end up on the trauma scale of parental death. Would I be able to keep a cool head if I was goaded by other kids, or would I end up breaking their noses like Kian had done. Wherever I landed, I knew I had them both there to support and help me fight my corner.

Grabbing my hand and pulling me up off of the spot I'd fallen asleep in, he ran towards the door of my bedroom.

"Everything's fine, but you need to come with me, quickly!"

With my hand placed in his, I followed behind him and flicked my eyes around the room. My bed remained freshly made from the day before, making me feel embarrassed for not sleeping in it for yet another night. The teddy that I'd been given by Grace—the lady who worked here—the first night I was bought back from the hospital, sat amongst the two blue and white striped cushions at the head of the bed. It was worn and one of the ears was slightly hanging off, and the cream bow around its neck was slightly discoloured and frayed at the ends.

She said the bear had superpowers – I knew it didn't, I wasn't a baby, but I could tell from her voice, and the way her eyes beamed when she spoke about it, that it was special, that maybe it belonged to someone who meant a lot to her.

Releasing myself from Kian's hand, I turned around and jogged over to the bed to grab the bear, I'd left it on the bed for the last few weeks. Maybe because I was surrounded by grown men who I aspired to be like and I didn't want to look like a baby. But for some reason I wanted it with me today, just like I did in the first few weeks that I arrived here, a comforter in the form of a worn-out old teddy. I wanted to be a kid again, and it was starting to become apparent to me that for so long I'd had to act years older than I really was.

"Tanner, hurry up! There's some big news dad wants to tell you." My ears pricked up and with the curiosity getting the better of me, I sprinted towards him, a queasiness starting to flare up in the pit of my stomach at what this big news was. Kian didn't seem to be worried about this *big* news, but the risk that it was something I wasn't going to like played on my mind the entire journey down the stairs.

Grabbing hold of the balustrade, I threw my leg over it, balancing on my stomach and sliding down the smooth dark oak until I reached the bottom, Kian chasing me on foot down the stairs. Jumping off the end, my heart raced at a crazy pace as I ran behind him, my legs almost long enough to keep up with his stride.

Dropping my head and slowing my run into a walk, a wave of despair suddenly hit me. What if I wouldn't be here to grow tall enough to beat him? What if I wouldn't be here to see Christmas this year or the year after that? What if I wasn't here long enough to see in my eleventh birthday next week? Biting my nails, I carried on following Kian into the kitchen and out through the double doors onto the patio. My heart sank when I saw who was waiting on the other side.

Betty.
Betty, the social worker.

My skin crawled as I saw her standing there next to Garrett, her silver hair highlighting the possibility that I might not be here for much longer, jeopardising my chance of happiness. With a briefcase in one hand and paperwork in the other, she looked like an orphan kid's nightmare. Revealing her crooked, coffee-stained fangs as she smiled at me, my blood ran cold and with the prospect of being put into the care system hanging over my head, anxiety crippled me.

"Ahh there he is! How have you been Tanner? Wow, aren't you getting big?" Betty pushed her hand through my hair, the need to tell her about this thing called personal space was too tempting. She'd only seen me a couple of weeks ago, so I found it hard to believe that I had grown enough for her to warrant making a comment about it.

Side stepping around her, I dragged my feet and made my way towards Garrett who was standing in between two small rose bushes either side of the wooden archway to the new section of garden he'd recently had completed.

Settling in front of him, I mentally prepared myself for the worst, I might only be young, but I wasn't stupid, I knew what might happen. No one had actually told me, but I'd heard enough of the conversations he and Betty had had about my guardianship. The care system was there for people like me, a support structure in place to help parentless kids find their *forever home*.

Over the last three months, Betty had tried to get me to see a child psychologist twice a week, not that I went often, and when I did, I hardly said a single word to the doctor. She tried to sell it to me as though it would be something to help me overcome the grief that had reared its ugly head as a result of my mum's death and the string of violent acts I'd endured at the hands of the men she had allowed into my life.

I never spoke about that side of my story to anyone, but it was obvious that I was physically harmed by someone when I got to the hospital. There was no way it would have gone unnoticed; my back was completely ripped to shreds from the belt that had been struck down on me that night and even now the scars were still there to prove the abuse.

I could feel Garrett's eyes draw down to me, but I couldn't bring myself to look at him, not when I could be taken away from him at any moment. Instead, I kept my eyes pinned to my hands picking along the bottom of the jumper I had on.

"It's okay son." Placing his hand on my shoulder, my torment was clearly obvious to him. Sighing out heavily, I couldn't help but open my mouth.

"Please don't make me go with her, I don't want to. I want to stay here with you guys. I'll do anything to stay here, I'll help Grace with cleaning the house." I paused, coming up for breath. "I promise I won't get angry or upset anymore. I'll even sleep in my bed instead of the wardrobe." I couldn't stop myself, and at this point I'd even go to stupid therapy. "P-please don't make me go."

Letting out an airy laugh, he tugged me tighter into his side.

"Tanner, you're not going anywhere, that's what I wanted to talk to you about." Lifting my gaze away from my hands, I peered up at him between my auburn hair, his steel blue eyes meeting mine.

"I-I'm not?"

"Oh my god dad, just tell him already, will you? You're killing us over here old man!" Kian yelled; his expression painted with anticipation, as if he was ready to burst from the excitement of whatever it was they all knew was coming.

Letting out a huff and waving his hand at Kian in a bid to calm him down, Garrett knelt down to my eye level, I don't know if he knew it, but when he did that, it made me feel safer, like he wasn't going to hurt me, and I trusted him more each time he carried out this small insignificant act.

"If it's okay with you..." He paused, breathing in deeply through his nose before exhaling sharply, his minty breath fanning my face. "If it's okay with you Tanner, I'd like to adopt you."

What the hell.

I stood there, my heart thrashing against my ribcage as I took in the words he'd just let out into the open. I wanted to ask him if he'd repeat them, just so I was sure I'd heard right, but I didn't want to risk him changing his mind and sending me away with Betty. My eyes brimming with tears, I wiped them away with the sleeve of my jumper, trying to hide them.

"I hope they're happy tears lad," he chuckled, his words lingering in the air. "So, what do you say?" He cautiously asked, awaiting my response.

He wants to adopt me.
I'm not going with Betty.
I'm not going into care.

"Yes!" I blurted out, without hesitation. "Yes, yes, yes!" The tears that had been forming in my eyes at the thought of being taken away, suddenly turned into tears of joy. "I want to stay here, with you and with my brothers. Please."

Garrett didn't say a word, instead he pulled me into the biggest hug I'd ever received in my entire life. I could hear his heart as my head snuggled into him, it reminded me of the day he'd found me; how I trained my focus on the rapid beating in his chest, how it beat that way because he'd found me battered and bruised and left in the cold, and there was an uncertainty as to whether I'd pull through or not.

Today it beat similarly to the morning he found me, but this time it beat like that for a different reason.

This time it was because he wanted to *keep* me.

Over Two Years Later

SEPTEMBER

Chapter Eight

I woke this morning feeling refreshed and ready to see what today would bring. This would be my last weekend before I started Oakland Academy, the private school I'd been enrolled in. The school that my two brothers had gone to prior to me attending.

Somehow, I'd managed to see through the last two years at primary school, even considering all the time in education I'd missed whilst I was dealing with everything that had gone on. I was proud of how far I'd managed to come in the last couple of years or so.

Dad had moved me to a different school once my adoption paperwork had been signed and finalised. The teachers there knew about what had happened, but they never questioned it, they just allowed me to carry on like any other normal kid.

It helped me to start a fresh, and secretly, so did the therapy I begrudgingly started going to. I fought to the bone about going, but it appears that the Lawson's are quite a persuasive family unit, and their flawless teamwork somehow managed to get me into Dad's office with Dr Leighton.

My first few sessions were awful, but I soon realised that it was harder holding onto all the trauma than it was to open up and speak to someone about it. It soon became apparent that not only did I need to go, but I actually enjoyed the meetings.

As weird as it was sharing the negative parts of my life with a stranger, having someone to talk to about all of the things I'd been through helped, with the guarantee that what I said to her would stay between her and I.

Each session I went to, I started unpicking the parts of my life that held all the demons locked away deep inside of me. Focusing on the reasons for my rage and frustration, eventually I stopped being filled with embarrassment and helplessness. Being able to pinpoint why I'd flip out and found it hard to regulate my emotions sometimes, assisted me in understanding the reasons I found it tricky, and what I could do to help identify the triggers before it got out of hand.

The more sessions I attended, the more I started to unravel a whole side of myself that I didn't know existed. I started to realise that I wasn't the way I was because I was a freak, like a few of the students in my class would call me. It wasn't anything to do with my genetics, I didn't get it from my mother or father, at least that's what the doc said. It was because of everything I'd gone through in my ten years on this planet, it was because of the unfortunate hand I had been dealt.

There was a valid reason for it. But you try to explain that to a stuck-up public-school kid with a perfect family and perfect life. Needless to say, it was easier said than done.

After months of therapy, I was able to go to school and not have the burning urge to punch Jimmy Curtis in the throat every time he looked at me funny. Instead, I attended my classes, focused on my work, and knuckled down to pass my end of school exams, coming top of my year group in every single subject.

I still had off days, but I was told that I was making excellent progress in dealing with this thing called PTSD, or whatever it was that the therapist said I had – *post trauma stressy* something or the other.

All I knew was that I owed it to Garrett to try and prove that it was worth him fighting to adopt me. He'd given me everything; all the fancy clothes, the tasty food that I had on my plate every night, the TV he had installed in my room, and without him, I would be in a care home with snotty toddlers running around, invading my personal space, and spluttering their germs all over me. Or even worse, I would have been found dead on that bench two and a half years ago.

Jogging down to the same bit of garden where I'd been asked to officially join the Lawson family, I looked up at the clear blue skies. There wasn't a cloud in sight, and the September morning sun heated my skin and warmed my soul.

Making my way under the archway, the rose bushes that had been planted there two years ago had grown so much since they were placed in the garden. It was poetic how much things could change in the space of two short years, the rose bushes mirroring the change and growth I'd seen in myself.

With each passing day, things seemed to start becoming clearer, my head wasn't as chaotic as before, my nightmares weren't as often, and I finally felt at peace with everything that had happened.

Moving towards the bench, I paused before sitting down and traced my fingertip over the embossed writing on the gold plaque which had been screwed onto it and made a mental note of how each of the letters felt under my touch.

Rose Campbell
May you dance forever amongst the flowers.

On the day that Garrett told me that he wanted to keep me and that I would be staying with him, he had men in to start working on something special for me. Not only did he adopt me, but he'd had a whole section of his garden redesigned off the back of some of the stories I'd told him about my mum being used for inspiration.

Roses for her name, and irises to represent her favourite flower, and in the centre of the area a large sundial, commemorating the time we'd spent out in the sun together – my favourite times.

Garrett was an incredible person, I don't know what I'd done to deserve being treated like this, but I would forever be in his debt.

Since I came back to the house after my stay in hospital, I'd always felt so comfortable being here, but as soon as the paperwork for my adoption was signed, sealed, and delivered to whoever the important person was that needed it, I actually felt at *home*.

Perching myself down on the bench that had been designed and handcrafted with complete care and precision, I listened to the birds chirping in the trees around the acres of land. Their songs gentle on my ears and strangely bringing me a sense of hope.

It was unexpectedly fulfilling to feel like that again, it was odd being able to freely feel safe and as though I belonged somewhere other than the only place I'd ever known.

Hell.

MARCH

Chapter Nine

The bell rang signalling the end of English with Mrs Clarke, she was an odd teacher—eccentric to say the least—with a love of books that I found quite endearing, but I liked her. She looked out for me without being overbearing, and she didn't put too much pressure on me if I was having an off day. I still had them every now and again, but they were nowhere near as bad as they used to be, and they were a lot less frequent. I had no idea why, but she just seemed to get me.

To be fair, all of the teachers were pretty kind, they seemed like they actually wanted to be here and teach the students rather than just looking at it as a pay day. And another bonus on top of the caring nature of the staff were the school lunches, which were a lot better than any stale sandwich that I got at Maple River Primary. But if I was being honest, I really hated it here at Oakland Academy.

For months now, Chad Durham had been picking on me and some of the other students, and I was getting sick of his stupid games. Sometimes I think that dealing with the men my mum used to bring home was easier than being in the same school as him and putting up with his bullying. He was cruel, not just to me, but to a lot of the other kids here as well, and I found it difficult to just sit back and witness everything that was going on, not that there was anything I could do to stop him.

Today, as I walked down the corridor in A Block, towards Mr. Harding's art classroom, I saw him tripping Brandon Carter over into a trophy cabinet, which resulted in him ending up in hospital with a face full of glass.

Brandon was one of my dad's friend's sons, we didn't really have much to do with each other and he'd never been round mine to play. His dad only ever came over to talk business, and even though I'd lived with them for two years, I still had no idea what it was they did. I never asked, I knew that sometimes it was better to stay quiet than to ask a bunch of questions only to be shut down.

Chad made me feel angry. He was bigger than everyone else in our year – and the majority of kids in the year above too. He reminded me so much of the men that would hurt me when I lived with my mum, which filled me with so many emotions. I wanted to protect myself and the others at school. I wanted to ram my fist into his face, but I didn't know how to throw a punch, and if I was to hit him, the likelihood that he'd get up and whack me ten times harder was pretty much a sure thing.

If I ever did hit him, I'd want it to hurt. It needed to, someone needed to put him in his place – and I wanted it to be me.

"Woah, what's wrong with you?" Dad teased as I slammed my bag down onto the counter of the kitchen worktop hard enough to make the cupboard doors underneath rattle.

Making my way around to the fridge to grab some fresh orange, I held my head down and tried to conceal the shiner that I'd been given on the way out from my last lesson of the day.

Yeah, *he* did it.

"Tanner, don't ignore me." He instructed, a seriousness in his voice I'd never heard before. I dropped my head, trying to pull myself together and find the courage to tell him about what had been going on at school. I didn't want him to think I was weak; my brothers could fight, they both boxed, and they were strong, especially Dax, he had muscles that would put some body builders to shame.

I was just a kid, I know that my body hadn't fully developed yet and that I shouldn't feel in competition with both of them, especially when they were a lot older than me, but I was impatient, and I longed to be like them right now. I knew that if I was then I could easily protect myself and all the other kids.

Grabbing the jug of orange out of the fridge, I squeezed my eyes tightly together before closing the door and showing my dad my bruised face. Giving him a quick flash of my face, I refused to make eye contact with him. I spun around and reached up to the top cupboard, remembering back to when I could barely reach it compared to now being able to open it with ease. Retrieving a glass, I noticed my dad pushing himself up off of the bar stool and pacing quickly over to where I was standing.

My initial reaction was to flinch when he stopped in front of me. I tightened my hands into fists by my sides ready to fight, even though my past occurrences of going to war with fully grown men seriously proved that I was unable to look after myself. I was still only a young boy, and there was no way in hell that I could protect myself.

I couldn't even protect myself from Durham.

My entire body seized up under the pretence that I'd landed myself in trouble with my adoptive father and I was about to pay for it. It had been a long time since I'd felt like I had to protect myself from an adult. I thought the therapy would have cleared the pre-set battle mode that had been programmed into me since I was younger, but it appears that it was still there, still ready to be activated if I needed to use it.

"Hey, it's okay," Dad reassured me, running his hand across my forehead, and pushing my tousled hair out of my face. Keeping my eyes tightly shut and trying to hold back the tears of frustration that filled behind them, I focused on my breathing in an attempt to calm myself down as best as I could.

In for four.
Out for four.

It was no good, I couldn't stay strong. I hated myself for not being like my older brothers. I despised the fact that I could do absolutely nothing about the bully at school. I was weak, just like I was when he had found me on that bench in the park, curled up and ready to give up on this thing called life.

Taking a step towards my father, my knees buckled underneath me, and I crumbled into his arms. But instead of letting me fall, he caught me.

He *caught* me.

"Dad, I-I can't do this a-anymore," I wept.

Christ, I sounded like a damn baby.

"Tanner, you need to tell me what's happening here. I don't know how to help you if I don't know what the problem is." He released me from his fatherly embrace, placing one hand on my shoulder and tipped my chin up with the other, forcing me to look at him.

With the tears in my eyes now uncontrollably streaming down my face, I breathed, focusing my attention on the man stood in front of me. There had been so many times since living here that made it clear that I wasn't on my own. I would never be left to fend or fight by myself by this man—my dad—who's presence initiated some kind of strength to shape itself dramatically inside me.

Sighing heavily and pulling myself together, I wiped away the wet from my cheeks, and stood tall in front of the person who had saved me two years ago. As hard as it was for me to ask people for help, I needed to. I needed to put this to bed.

"Dad, I need your help. Please." I asked, knowing full well that he would do anything for those people he loved.

"Just tell me what it is. Are you in trouble kid? Has something happened at school? It's okay if it has, you're not going to be told off." He rambled, tripping over his words. The tone of his voice made it evident that I mattered a great deal to him, as if I was his own flesh and blood, as if the piece of paper he'd signed on the day of my adoption was exactly that, nothing more than just a silly bit of paper.

This man didn't have a bad bone in his body, and quite frankly, I couldn't imagine him hurting a fly, let alone me. I'd never seen him become aggressive toward or raise his voice at my two brothers. He was one of the gentlest people I had ever encountered, which I suppose wasn't hard considering the long list of destructive people I'd been unfortunate enough to meet over my small number of years on this planet.

"No. Well, I mean, yes." I shook my head, my face

burning in frustration, annoyed at myself for being unable to spit the words out clearly enough for him to understand.

"Come on, let's go for a walk. Get your coat on." He ushered towards the coat pegs on the wall by the patio doors at the other end of the kitchen. Although it was bright for this time of year, there was a slight chill in the air, just like the one that made my skin prick whenever I walked into Oakland each day.

Shrugging on my black parker coat and zipping it up to my chin, I trailed behind my dad into the garden until I positioned myself next to him, falling in line with his stride. We stayed in silence for a while, our footsteps on the gravel the only noise filling the spring air. I knew where we were going—down to my mother's bench—Dad knew this was where I did all my thinking.

"Right, let's start at the beginning, talk to me so I can help you."

So that's exactly what I did.

Chapter Ten

Working the punch bag, the sweat dripped off of my brow and onto the mats below. Since our conversation a few weeks ago, dad had sent me to box with my two older brothers. He understood the need that I had to protect myself. He knew what I'd been through, he got it, and I was grateful for that. Luckily, I had these three male figures in my life. They had taught me so much over the last couple of years, and now they were teaching me the one thing I needed to know more than anything.

How to protect myself.

Training and being given hints and tips from Dax and Kian, improved my ability to protect myself, and fight whenever I needed to. I had an undeniable sense of security and power now. Obviously, it was less than likely that I'd be able to take down a fully grown man if I ever needed to—not yet anyway—but it gave me the courage to stand up to bullies my own age, which was exactly what I was going to do.

Durham had continued to pick on the same kids in my year group at school, some confrontations worse than others, a lot of them were probably secretly thankful that all they were subjected to was a juice box over their head, and not an unplanned trip to the emergency department.

Until dad had explained, I couldn't understand how, in such a prestigious institution, a boy like Durham could remain there. The private school proudly boasted about the values it upheld, with posters stuck up on the walls of the classrooms and in brochures spread out in the reception area for visitors to take away. They were values that a lot of other state schools in the area couldn't offer.

In my eyes, having someone like him walking freely through the halls of Oakland Academy made the school just as bad as the ones where the kids would have to walk through security detectors to ensure that none of the students were carrying weapons.

Of course, his parents had money, enough to buy the silence of the school and have them turn a blind eye to the bullying that was going on. I don't know what made me angrier, his parents, Durham's bullying, or the fact the school were being paid to keep their mouths shut.

Regardless, it was wrong whichever way you looked at it, and it fuelled me enough to work hard at school, steer clear from Durham and practice every evening with my brothers at MT Boxing, the gym they went to.

Dax, who had nearly marched himself down to the school when he found out what had been going on, had to argue his case with the manager of the business to get him to let me train there. The lessons he ran started from aged fourteen, he wasn't happy letting me attend them, something to do with health and safety and insurance. I needed to get started as soon as I could, I needed to sort Durham out as quick as possible, the idea that he was able to use the school as his own personal playground orchestrated a rush of havoc with the ever-growing anxiety that built up inside of me.

Leaning on the side of the boxing ring, I'd listened in on my brother's conversation with the owner, fighting my corner as always.

"What if he trained with me? I promise, you won't even know he's here. He needs to do this Murph. Do you understand what kind of life he's had, and now he's being fucking bullied at school? Jesus Christ, you need to let me bring him here, you need to let me teach him how to protect himself.

This Durham kid is a fucking savage, man – a terrorist... Do you know how many of the students have ended up in hospital because of these so-called accidents the school's said they've been in? One was pushed down two flights of stairs and broke his arm and three of his goddamn ribs! Adrian Carter's kid, Brandon, the poor lad had his head put through the trophy cabinet...

Your face is saying it all man, come on, please...

He needs this...

The other kids need him to do this."

There was no denying it took some persuading, but eventually, Murph gave into my eldest brother's begging and negotiated with him, agreeing to let him train me out the back where I wouldn't be seen, then once I turned fourteen, I'd be able to enrol in the proper classes at MT Boxing.

He'd been coaching me hard, every day after school in the back of the gym, and even at home, making sure I got in as many hours as possible. My birthday was now only a couple of weeks away, and soon enough I'd be able to train and fight in the ring with kids my own age.

Durham was twice the size of me though, which is why

training with my brothers came in handy. They were even bigger than the brute gracing the school corridors. If I could land a blow to them, then Durham would be easy – at least I hoped.

I had speed and agility on my side, he was big boned and slow with his movements, which is probably why he resorted to pushing kids down flights of stairs and ramming their heads into glass cabinets. The damage he inflicted on them was never through a proper punch up, just one solid attack, catching them off guard and serving a killer blow.

"That's it kiddo, you've got that combo down." Kian shouted from behind the boxing pads he was holding. "Again! Two-three-two!" I mustered up all the energy I had left in me by the end of our ninety-minute session.

Cross.
Left hook.
Cross.

Dax had told me that this combo could land me some powerful impact punches which would leave Durham knocked senseless. He would never be quick enough to block the punches, he was too sluggish, and having the knocks coming from different angles would more than likely confuse him. There was no way he'd be able to keep up with me.

Rotating my hips as I threw the last two punches, I could feel the power transfer from my legs, up through my body and into my wrapped fists. Ducking as Kian countered me with one of the pads, I landed the final punch on the front of the other, hard enough that it sent him stumbling backwards.

"Yes, Tanner! That's what I'm talking about!" The thrill in my brother's voice, made the swelling on my knuckles worth it. "Just you wait until this Durham prick starts, he's not going to know what's hit him." He growled as he made his way to the stairs and up to the secret entrance. I sat down on the floor and started to remove the tape from around my wrists, filling my lungs with as much oxygen as possible, trying to catch my breath.

"Yo, Dax, get your ass down here man!" Bellowing at the top of his lungs, it wasn't long until my eldest brother appeared from behind the makeshift doorway positioned in the hallway upstairs and paced down the wooden stairs into the basement.

"Well, damn." Dax said wide-eyed as he flicked his gaze between the blood-stained hand wraps on the floor and my knuckles.

"He's ready."

SEPTEMBER

Chapter Eleven

As I made my way through the grand entrance of Oakland Academy, it seemed almost surreal that I was starting my second year of secondary school. Looking back on the last few years, it was crazy to think about just how much had happened, everything I'd been through and all the progress I'd made in my life since I was found on that bench in Highpoint Park.

I had a family now, a *real* family. A family who recognised and treated me as one of their own. A dad and two brothers who would fight to the death for me, dealing with any and all consequences that came along with it. I missed my mum every day, but being with them made me question everything I knew before this life. I was better off here, I was cared for and looked after, I was fed and clothed, but most of all, I was safe.

This year felt different, over the summer break something had clicked inside of me. I'd shot up a good few inches, and the training I had been doing had given me both the physical and mental strength I needed, not only to stand up for myself and the other school kids, but also to be able to deal with whatever future curveballs life decided to throw in my direction. If my past was anything to go by, then there was more than likely going to be a few more of those. I was ready to take on the next year, the good and the bad, the friends *and* the bullies.

I was ready to take on Chad Durham.

The bell echoed through the corridor that linked the English and science buildings together, and that's when I heard him. The voice that had haunted the kids here at Oakland since we started here last year, and the voice that the new students here would also become afraid of.

Slamming the door to my locker shut and turning the key to secure it, I spun myself around to see Durham snaking his way down towards me, shoving past the kids who hadn't been quick enough to move out of his way on their own accord.

Stand tall, Tanner.

My brother's voice resounded in my head, repeating the words he'd said to me before Hank had dropped me off this morning.

You've got this.

Holding my ground, I observed the school terrorist barging through the crowded hallway and I kept my gaze on him. He didn't have any associates, he worked alone, he was big enough to. He didn't need the support of any of the other students here. In a way I guess it being like that worked in our favour, we only had to deal with him, and him alone was more than enough for us to manage.

"Well, look who it is." Durham growled, baring his teeth, stopping a few feet away from me and gazing down at Brandon, a fire burning so dark in his eyes it could put hell to shame.

He looked completely and utterly terrified standing

there alone shifting his weight underneath his feet and looking down at the floor. Refusing to make eye contact with the aggressor posed in front of him; I couldn't blame him, the last time he'd come to knocks with Durham, he'd ended up with a face full of glass and stitches on his forehead leading from his eyebrow up to his hairline.

Not today, Durham. Not today.

My feet started moving before I could process what I was going to do next, my act completely unplanned, all I knew was that today was the start of a new future for myself and the other Oakland students.

Today was the day that I was going to take down Durham.

Chapter Twelve

I STARED down at the blood.

What have I done?

Crimson had already begun to dry, and bruising had started to appear around my swollen hands. Something had happened, and considering the amount of blood there was, it was something bad.

It wasn't all mine, my knuckles were split, but I knew from the amount of training I'd done with my brothers, that they weren't damaged enough to warrant this amount of blood. It was everywhere, across my hands, up my arms, and splattered across the white school shirt that I wore.

What if I've killed someone?

Sitting alone outside of the headteacher's office, the unnerving silence occupied the long hallway. There was no one in sight, no noises coming from the adjoining rooms. It was like I was in a dream, one where you know something had happened but couldn't quite recall what. One of those dreams that made a sombre anxiousness settle in the pit of your stomach.

I sat still, focusing all of my energy on trying to

remember, struggling to put together the pieces of what had taken place.

Oh, God. Please don't let me have killed someone.

A granular cough broke me from my concentration, a cough that I knew.

Dax.

"Alright Kiddo?" He smirked, ruffling my hair as he took a seat in the plush cream velvet chair next to me. I didn't respond, my stomach knotted, twisting itself inside out with the overwhelming sense of fretfulness that pumped through me.

"Tanner." Dax snapped, his tone firmer.

I'd killed someone. I knew it.

Releasing a shaky breath, I forced myself to turn my head and look at him. I didn't want to be in trouble. I didn't want to face what was coming. I couldn't get the notion out of my head that I'd done something unforgiveable.

"Have I k-killed someone?" My bottom lip started to wobble. There was no other reason for the amount of blood that was smeared on me. Dax's mouth parted and his eyes shot wide open, before letting out the most sobering laugh I think I'd ever heard. One that I needed to hear, just for some kind of confirmation that I indeed, *hadn't* killed someone.

"No, Tanner, you haven't *killed* anyone."

"I h-haven't?" I could have cried when I knew that I wouldn't be locked away and punished for murder. I knew I wasn't a murderer, but I couldn't shake the thought from my mind, especially when I couldn't remember a damn thing.

"No, you definitely haven't, but you are in trouble. Well, with the headteacher anyway." I gulped, trying to swallow down the sicky feeling rising in my throat. I'd never gotten myself into any bother at school, even when everything had gone tits up in my earlier years, I'd always tried my best and stayed away from drama.

Durham.

"Let's just say, in trouble with Mr. Barton or not, you're going to be a fucking hero when you return to school after your suspension." Dax chuckled before standing up, waiting for me to follow his lead into the headteacher's office.

Chapter Thirteen

My stomach churned fiercely as Hank pulled up the gravel path towards the stately house. Even now, some days I still found it bizarre that I got to call this place home. I was going to be in so much trouble with dad.

Fiddling with my blood-stained school shirt I thought about a million and one things that I could say to dad to get him to see it from my point of view.

I'd pretty much battered Durham to mush, his face was beaten and bruised. I'd broken his nose, and when he tried to fight back, I broke his wrist as well. As soon as I heard the account of events recited back to me by Mr Barton, it was like a switch inside of me was flicked on, and everything came flooding back. Every single memory, every feeling of every punch that made contact with his skin. I remembered it all.

He deserved it.

He was about to hurt Brandon.

Again.

He could have hurt him even worse than last time, and we all know how that ended up. I vowed that when I returned to school in the new term that I would do everything I could to protect myself and the other students, which is exactly what I'd been training to do. Except maybe, I could have stopped after the second punch that landed him on his ass. But no, I had to carry on, I didn't hold back, I didn't think to stop when I could feel his bones snapping in my grasp, or his skin splitting underneath my knuckles.

My judgement turned into a hazy mist of red, a mirage of all the pain and suffering I'd not only seen in the walls of the school, but of all the damage I'd experienced when I was younger as well. The intensity of anger and torment came rushing back, intoxicating my senses like a nightmare, and taking over my body as though I'd become possessed by a demon.

There was no way in hell I was sorry for what I'd done, everyone knew he had it coming, and the only thing I was sorry for was not doing it sooner. If only I'd reached out for help last year, I could have put an end to all this before it got so out of hand. Even though I was scared to death of what my dad was going to say, I couldn't help but be proud of what I'd done.

I'm going to be a hero. A real-life hero.

Stopping the Range Rover with a force hard enough for my seatbelt to lock, Hank turned to me as if he was going to say something, but he didn't. It was a weird drive home, usually he'd speak to me about football or joke with me asking if I had a girlfriend at school—*gross*—but today was different.

When Dax showed up at school, I thought that I might have been going home with him, but after receiving my two-week suspension from school—a lighter sentence than I thought I'd be slapped with—I was loaded up with textbooks and sent on my way off of the school's premises.

Dax said he had to go back to work, he'd said he'd only come up because dad was stuck in an important meeting which he couldn't get out of. In the back of my mind, I knew that wasn't the case, he was the boss, he could do what he wanted.

My brain went into overdrive, thinking that it was because he was so annoyed at me, that he couldn't calm himself down enough to come up to the school to sit in Mr Barton's office and listen to this morning's accounts.

He probably blamed Dax for persuading him to let us train together, and that alone was enough to let a sea of guilt drown me. It wasn't his fault; he was only trying to help me. God knows if I was in his position, I would have done the exact same thing as he did. We were family, and we stuck together.

Unclipping my seatbelt and reaching for the backseat doorhandle, I almost fell out of the car as Hank yanked it open for me, another suspect move on his part. I grabbed my school bag from the footwell of the car before jumping out and chucking it over my shoulder sheepishly.

"Is everything okay, Hank?" Something seemed off, but I couldn't quite put my finger on it. Studying me for what felt like an uncomfortable length of time, the stern look that usually sat on his face suddenly dispersed and a faint smile tore away in the corners of his mouth.

"W-What?" I snorted under my breath.

"You remind me so much of your father." *Huh?* "It's nice to watch you grow up and find your own place in this family." He put a hand on my shoulder, and I was sure for a second, that he was about to pull me into a bear hug.

"You mean, you're not mad at me?"

"No way kid, no way in hell could I be mad at you, not that it would be *my* place to be. I just know what that piece of shit was like, your dad told me." Stopping himself and turning slightly red at the fact he'd said *shit* in front of me, he released my shoulder from under his hand.

"He deserved it, Hank, and honestly, if I could do it again, then I would. No questions asked." I said, backing myself and standing up proud, pleased that I'd been the one to protect someone for once in my damn life.

"I know you would, that's why I'm... well, I guess, I'm proud of you." Stumbling over his words, he shifted on his feet. "I've seen you go from that boy on the bench, to the boy who's standing in front of me now, the boy that is slowing turning into a man." I blushed at his words and tried viciously to blink away the tears forming in my eyes. I wasn't going to cry, like Hank just said, I was turning into a man. Men don't cry.

Awkwardly, I gave Hank a smile and shuffled past him in a bid to escape the overwhelming sense of pride he'd just given me. I wasn't used to feeling this good about myself, it was alien to me.

With the gravel crunching underneath my feet as I made my way towards the front door, I heard Hank shout out at me.

"And by the way Tanner." Turning around to see him stood there with his hands against his mouth, "I've done this exact same journey with both of your brothers!"

Chapter Fourteen

The last two weeks had gone by in a flash and before I knew it, I was walking back through the doors of Oakland and about to hand in the assignments that had been set for me to complete during my hiatus from school.

Dad had been pretty chilled about the whole ordeal, backhandedly congratulating me for sticking up for Brandon. I mean, how could I not have stuck up for him? I had been trained to do that and given the resources to help me accomplish what I'd done. My brothers had high-fived me and asked for all of the details to the story, not that they mentioned it in front of dad, he was giving them both the cold shoulder; apparently, they trained me too much and taught me things that I didn't need to know, not that any of us three cared. My brothers cared even less than I did.

After a few days, the atmosphere between my dad and brothers cleared and everything was back to normal, minus me being able to box, my hands were in tatters and it hurt to pick up a pen, let alone hit a pad. Dad had told me he could have bought me a computer to do my work on, but he thought that the pain from writing with my injured hands might be a good lesson in knowing when to stop.

As I jogged up the concrete steps and towards the grand wooden doors of the school foyer, my body started to crawl with the same nervousness that struck me on the journey home from school after receiving my suspension. Placing my hand on the door, I froze on the spot, my legs unable to move.

What if they didn't think I was a hero like Dax said they would? What if they all thought I was a bully, just like Durham? Everything I had trained for and did was for all of our safety and I wished with every fibre of my being, that they would see it the same way I did.

I breathed in deeply and prepared myself for what was to come next, before pushing open the doors and stepping into the hallway where I knew students would be gathering, probably waiting for my arrival. The door felt as heavy as my heart did, and when I made my way through, the sensation of everyone's eyes falling on me made me wish that my suspension had been another six months longer than it had been, just enough time for there to have been some other sort of drama here so they'd forget about what I'd done two weeks ago.

With students turning around and stopping in their tracks, whispers filled the main lobby. I dropped my head, focusing on the tiled floor below me and scurried through the statue crowds, sensing them eyeballing me even more than they already had been.

It was intimidating, and a bit freakish, the same feeling I got when I walked down one of the hallways at home that housed all these old paintings, the feeling of being watched by the old people in each of the portraits that were hung on the walls. There were so many eyes on me it was unnerving.

I needed to get out of here. Pulling my school bag up onto my shoulder more, I dropped my head and started to head towards the headteacher's office, eyes following me as I dipped between the students.

Before I had a chance to get to the door at the other end of the room, a slow applause began to fill the area, I don't know who started it, but it was initiated by one single clap. Then another, and another, and within seconds, all of the students who were stood there staring at me had joined in. It was a dramatic reaction, like I'd just arrived back from war where I'd beaten the enemy. And to be honest, I guess that's exactly what I'd done.

I was *David* in this story, and Durham had been demoted to *Goliath*.

I'd never been so dumbfounded, I didn't know what to do, or what to say, and although I was slightly embarrassed by all of the attention, it felt good. I felt *good*.

Students started moving towards me, greeting me with pats on the back and high-fives, and I felt like a god damn celebrity, all I needed now was a news crew, flashing lights and a camera pointed in my face. I swear I hadn't even seen half of these kids before, but clearly, they had either; one been a victim of Durham's or two; they'd heard everything about him and what I'd done to drastically try and defuse the bullying that was going on. Whatever it was, they all seemed happy for me to be returning to the school.

When I left for my suspension, Mr Barton had made it clear that I could only return to the school once it had been raised in the parent and student council meetings. If they voted that I wasn't a threat to the rest of the students, then I would be allowed to return after two weeks, on the other hand, if they believed that I posed a danger, then I'd be out.

It was a long wait and I felt as though I was waiting to

see if I was about to be executed for my wrongdoings, but the relief I felt when my dad told me I could return was like the big rock that had been slowly suffocating me for the entire time I'd been off had finally smashed into a thousand fragments.

I knew I wasn't a danger, and so did my dad and brothers, but the notion of potentially having my future at Oakland being ripped away from me as the decision was left down to a vote of students and parents was unbearable. None of the parents knew me, and I didn't even know the kids who would ultimately have the casting vote on whether they thought I still belonged there.

So, when dad got the call, the relief was indescribable. But even though I knew my future had been positively decided by a group of strangers, I still had doubts about how I'd be greeted on the day I returned to school.

Now I was back here, it was clear that people had seen what I did as a good thing, something that needed to be done in order to protect them and their kids from a ferocious bully that had made the lives of a lot of the students there a living hell. It had also come to light, that Durham's dad was paying the school to keep quiet, so an investigation had been opened into the management of the school. Mr Barton had been sacked with immediate effect, along with the deputy head teacher and a few of the other school board members. I didn't understand the ins and outs of it all, and quite frankly, I didn't really give a toss.

All I knew was that we had won.
We would be safe.
Brandon would be safe.
I would be safe.
Durham wasn't coming back to Oakland, that was a sure factor in this novel. His father's money couldn't keep

him here anymore, not when the police stepped in. No doubt, there would be other bully's that would walk through the doors, but for as long as I was there, I hoped that my name, and my story would keep them at bay, and I prayed that once I'd left, there would be someone like me to stand up for those kids who were too scared to stand up for themselves.

The students here were now a union, we were a tribe, and I felt like their leader.

Three Years Later

Chapter Fifteen

Shooting some hoops with Brandon after school, we planned to stop off at Woody's for some pizza like we did every Friday night before heading home. I still wasn't quite sure on what I wanted to do with my future, but I knew that if I never made it in life, I'd have a job here. In god's honest truth, it wouldn't be the worst thing to happen either.

The pizza was incredible, and the staff were like a family, the atmosphere was always so welcoming, and it was a pretty cool place. It had vintage posters adorning the walls, and a classic black and white chequered flooring and retro orange sofas that matched the logo painted on the back wall. That's why we spent so much time hanging out here, it was eclectic and trendy, and the pizza was the best I'd ever eaten. We were regulars, and secretly, the owner would always make sure our food came out before anyone else's, even if they'd ordered before us.

"You know something bro? When I was in the shower the other day, I had a thought." Brandon said mid mouthful.

"If you say the thought was about me whilst you were washing your dick, I'm going to murder you right here." I gagged, nearly spraying my drink over the table and onto Brandon's Hawaiian.

Never have been a pineapple on pizza kind of guy.
Never will be a pineapple on pizza kind of guy.
Fucking sociopath.

"Ha fucking ha. Who put fifty pence in the dickhead?" He choked, taking another bite out of his unhinged choice of toppings. "Seriously though, I never thanked you."

"Thanked me for what?" I cocked an eyebrow at him. I hadn't gotten him anything, I hadn't let him beat me at basketball recently, so his comment came accompanied by a side of complete confusion.

"For sticking up for me and putting that Durham cunt in the hospital." He scoffed before taking a well needed sip of his drink. I deadpanned him. We'd never spoken about this. Like, never *ever* spoken about this.

"You don't have to thank me for that, he had it coming to him, we all know that." I thought back to the discomfort I experienced in the hallway on the day I was allowed to return back to school after my altercation with *Goliath* and tried to steer away from anymore heroics being thrown my way.

"Well, I am. So, I'd accept it, because from now on I'm not thanking you for another fucking thing." Sticking his middle finger up at me he went back to tuck into another slice.

Three years ago, Brandon and I formed a friendship that was unbreakable, I don't even remember how it happened, but it just did. I was thankful for it though, it made me feel *normal* when I returned back to Oakland, he didn't come at me with a teary-eyed Oscar worthy speech, hell he'd never even muttered the words *thank you* – not that I wanted an apology. Not from him. Not from anyone. I didn't even think I deserved one, I just did what needed to be done.

The bond we had was like the one I had with my younger cousin Lily. Lily was the daughter of my adoptive fathers brother, but I loved the high-spirited thirteen-year-old as if she was a product of my own bloodline. The thing was with Brandon, Lily and I, was that we just got each other. Everything made sense when we were all together, and we knew what each of us were thinking just by looking at each other, we didn't need words to communicate, we just *knew*.

It was nice to have a relationship like that with someone, and I was lucky enough to have two of those in my life. Before I lived in this world I do now—when there was nothing but my messed-up childhood—if you'd have asked someone who'd known what my life was like back then, they would have said I didn't have a hope in hell, that I wouldn't make anything of myself, and I'd only end up becoming a loser, or worse off, dead. Luckily, I'd managed to flip that notion on the head and prove all of those people wrong.

This fucker who was sat opposite me, chewing demonically on an equally as demonic choice of pizza, had grown to become like a brother to me. Sure, I still had Dax and Kian, but they were a lot older than me, they didn't want to do the things I wanted to do, like shoot hoops and eat greasy foods in a brightly painted diner. They had their own lives, their own jobs, and other more important responsibilities to take care of, and I got that. They knew that I could look after myself now, without having to run to them for help every five minutes.

I understood that over time, we wouldn't be how we were when I first joined the family. They had done so much for me over the last few years, they'd taken this little weed of a boy and taught him things, they helped me grow and I would be forever grateful for them. It went without saying, I knew I could still go to them if I was ever in trouble, or needed advice, but they weren't Brandon.

People say about soul mates, people that are meant for each other, and how they find each other in this world. They're *destined*. Well, this idiot was my soul mate, that's the only way I could describe it. Not that we'd ever say that to each other, he'd call me out on my poetic bullshit, and I'd slap him round the head for it, but I knew it, and he knew it – just like Lily did. We had each other, no matter what life threw at us. We were bound to one another, and that was enough for us all in this crazy fucking world.

"Lil not coming today?" Brandon asked raising an eyebrow and pushing his empty plate away from him and into the centre of the table. It made me laugh internally at how different he was now compared to three years ago. He had a sense of cocky arrogance about him, one that oddly suited him.

"Yeah, she was meant to be. Maybe she's got held up, I know she had dance after school, but Leonard was meant to be dropping her here once she was done." Unease filled my chest; it was unlike her to miss our Friday pizza nights at Woody's. She *never* missed our Friday pizza nights.

"C'mon, let's go look for her."

Six Months Later

Chapter Sixteen

"Who did this to you?" I questioned my baby cousin. "Honestly Lil, heads are going to fucking roll tomorrow when I get to school." I roared as I barged into her room uninvited, after hovering in the doorway and watching her sob for the last ten minutes.

"Tanner, I'm fine, it doesn't matter, please j-just –"

"Don't. Don't even tell me to drop it. I'm going to fucking kill them. Now, tell me who it is so I can sort them out."

Wiping the tears away, she stared up at me with her ocean blue eyes, willing me not to cause a drama. Something I found impossible to do when it was affecting my younger cousin the way it was. Her short black bob looked the opposite of how she always wore it, brushed to perfection – she always carried a hairbrush around in her bag with her, she told me the needed to brush it at least three times a day for it to keep the way it did. Now though, it was an untamed masterpiece, like a piece of abstract art hanging up on show for the world to see in a brightly lit gallery. Colours thrown onto a canvas with no real direction or indication of what it was meant to be. That's how I saw Lil now, messy, and unrecognisable.

"Okay, fine. You don't have to tell me, but I swear to God Lil, if—*when*—I find out who made you so upset, that's it for them."

This wasn't the first time I'd heard Lily crying in her room. Over the last six months, things with Lily had gone from bad to worse. She was thirteen years old, and I'd heard her bawling her eyes out pretty much every day I'd been round to my aunt and uncle's house. She was acting like she was a heartbroken teenager and whatever was going on was the end of the world in her eyes. Nothing any of us said or did made the slightest bit of difference, even the tub of *Ben & Jerry's* I'd picked up from the shop for her. Ice cream is meant to be good for heartbreak, right?

I was worried for her, and concerned that when I finished Oakland at the end of the year she'd be left on her own at the school, without me or Brandon there to look after her. I just didn't understand what was going on, at school she was popular, she was excelling in every single subject up until recently, and she was a fucking brilliant ballet dancer. The girl had it all, she was a triple threat, but something was going on, and it pained me not to know how I could help her.

Storming out of her room and swinging myself around the balustrade of the staircase, I made for my aunt's kitchen, hoping to get some answers to my cousin's odd behaviour. I didn't know where I was going to find them, but I needed to do something, I hated seeing her like this, especially when I could possibly do something to rectify the issue.

My bet was on the new kid that had started in her year at school. Some jumped up, self-entitled prick who seemed to think that, even at the age of thirteen, he ruled the school, and all of the students in it. I'd dealt with people like him before. I'd dealt with Durham, and this kid didn't even come close to him in comparison. I'd never seen this new kid use his fists to hurt anyone else, but he was sly and sneaky, and I didn't fucking like him.

Trailing through the hallways with my eyes bolted to the floor, I wracked my brains planning a way in which I could get to the bottom of this saga and get Lily back to the person she was six months ago. My frustration grew deeper, my temper unhealthier, and even though I didn't know for sure if the new kid was to blame for Lily's sudden change in character, I wanted to punch him square in the face; if for nothing other than to take my anger out on something more than just an inanimate object.

Without warning, I was met by a brick wall. The brick wall of Leonard's torso; Lily's driver was another one of my dad's right-hand men. Another person I didn't fucking like.

"Woah, slow it down there, cowboy!" He grinned, baring his chipped front tooth. I don't know why but teeth grossed me out to such a dramatic level, maybe it reminded me of Betty's gnashers, but every time that Leonard smiled, I wished that he hadn't.

"Sorry. Didn't see you there." I said, standing straight and lifting my chin up. I wasn't as tall as him, but he walked with such a bad posture, that it made me reconsider walking around hunched over like I had been.

"You need to get your head out your ass there, Tanner. You never know who you're going to bump into."

Ha-fucking-ha.

He always had a way of making a diggy comment sound as though he was joking. I didn't really like the prick, but he was my dad's friend, so I bit my tongue and tolerated him on the occasions we were in the same room as each other.

Maybe, just maybe, I could punch him instead.

As though he could read my mind, he levelled his spine and puffed out his chest, proving he was bigger than I was, and looked down at me, almost threatening me to say or do something.

You don't stand a chance.
He would flatten you, Tanner.
Don't be an idiot.

Remembering why I'd been so riled up in the first place, I decided to use this encounter to do some digging, maybe he'd have some useful information. I doubted it, but it was worth a shot.

"Do you know what's wrong with Lily? Has she said anything to you?" I asked bluntly.

"What do you mean, what's wrong with Lily?"

Jesus, it doesn't take a fucking genius to see how tore up she is over whatever is going on. Surely, he's noticed the change in her behaviour. How could he not have?

Prick.

"She's upset. All the time, Leonard." Using his name for effect I carried on the interrogation. "You must have seen that something's not right with her. You drive her to and from school every single day, you take her to her extra curriculars."

"Nothing is wrong with her."

"But –"

"Nothing. Is. Wrong." His eyes bore into me, darkening, swearing me off from asking anymore questions.

Jeez. This guy creeps me out.

"Fine. Whatever, thanks for the help." I responded, noticeably rolling my eyes at him before walking away in the direction I'd been heading in.

One Year Later

Chapter Seventeen

Returning home from college early, the house seemed exceptionally quiet.

Deadly, quiet.

Unless everyone was asleep, there was always some kind of hustle and bustle here; conversations between my father and his business partners, or the loud cheering—or cursing—from my brothers and their friends as they watched whatever sport was showing on the television. Today was different, maybe it was because I wasn't usually home this early, but something didn't quite sit right with me.

After finishing at the school last year, I enrolled in the Academy's sixth-form college, just so I could keep an eye out on Lily. The Business Management course that I was doing was teaching me fuck all. I didn't even want to do it, and remaining a prisoner there felt unbearable. I just wanted to spread my wings, be done with Oakland and see what the next chapter of my life brought me, but I couldn't leave.

Not whilst Lily was still there.

I *had* to do it.

I *had* to stay.

I *had* to make sure she was safe.

I chucked my keys onto the maple wood unit in the foyer of the house, noticing that the noise from the metal hitting the wood and my footsteps were the only sounds echoing through the corridors, and I swear I could hear my heart drumming away in my chest. Grace wasn't even around, and she had always been there at the front door pretty much every day since I'd started going to Oakland.

Lily wasn't at school again today, which was becoming a regular occurrence, she'd blown out of all of her classes and hadn't danced for over a year, needless to say the shot of getting a scholarship at the city's best dance academy was out the window now. This got to me more than anything else, and that's why I knew that this was something more than just a dickhead boy or bitchy girl at school. It was something bigger than she was letting on.

Lily always told me that dancing was her nirvana. Whenever she was having a rough time, all she had to do was put on some music and her pointe shoes and she felt... *free*. But she'd dropped it completely; she was no longer dancing, and I could tell that she was no longer free. Instead of carrying her pastel pink ballet bag on her shoulder, she was carrying a weight on her shoulders, a weight heavy enough to warrant her cutting off her family completely.

I could tell by the look in her washed out and dark ringed eyes, that she was trapped in her body, just living miserably, unwilling to tell anybody what was hurting her. All I wanted was for her to talk to us, to someone, to *me*.

We'd always been so close; I loathed the fact that there was now something going on in her life that was able to build up a steel rodded concrete barricade between us. A barricade I couldn't smash down. I'd given her space and pressed her for some kind of information about what was going on, but nothing seemed to work, whatever I did, she remained quiet and distant.

"Hello?" I shouted out, the husk in my voice bouncing off of the walls. I'd travelled down these corridors so many times before now, but for some unbeknown reason, today it all felt a little too strange, a tidal wave of panic and unease crashed through my body.

No one answered, so I called out again and made my way towards the office that my father was usually sat in when I came home from college. Maybe he was having a meeting and Grace was making them drinks in the kitchen. Still, a thick smog of uncertainty seemed to bleed through the hallways.

Heading towards the west wing of the house, I finally heard voices. They were muffled, and I couldn't work out what was being said, but at least it was something. I hadn't been left alone and abandoned again – not that my dad and brothers would leave this place. With this information the disturbing atmosphere started to lift, my nerves and concerns evaporating from the pit of my stomach.

Well, at least for a split second they did.

Until I heard the screams.

The distressing cries of a man coming from the hidden entrance of the basement. The room I'd spent so much time in with my brothers practicing my boxing and fitness. I ran down the two adjoining passageways in record time, getting there as fast as I could, I knew this route like the back of my hand.

My stomach filled with that feeling you get when you know something bad is about to happen, shadowy butterflies fluttered around in my belly as I swallowed down my fear, trying to shake away this unexplainable feeling. What if something had happened to my dad or my brothers? Surely there wasn't a person dumb enough in this country to break in and hurt them.

Pulling out the panelling, the secret doorway behind was unlocked. It was *never* unlocked.

Since I started training, I'd tried to get in there on numerous occasions, not to snoop around, but because I wanted to get some extra time in on the bag. Each time I'd failed. The door had been deadbolted, no soul was getting in there unless they had the key. Which I didn't.

One time I got caught by Dax; I was sat on the floor trying desperately to pick the lock with a hair pin I'd nicked from Lily's bedroom. Unfortunately, my master plan didn't work, and it soon became apparent that I'd never make it as a low life criminal.

The inaudible sound of voices developed into a language that I could understand, although still low, the hushed words were suddenly interjected by more alarming cries.

What the fuck is going on.

I pushed through the entrance, placing my hands on either side of the walls to steady myself as I made it down the wooden stairs. Normally, I'd pull the string to my right and allow the room to be flooded by the bright LED lights fitted into the ceilings – but something told me that now was certainly not the time to be doing so.

The floorboards of the rickety stairs creaked beneath me, and I questioned why, with all the money my father had in his pockets, he hadn't installed a proper staircase, or at least one that didn't make you think you were going to snap your neck falling down it.

The smell of sweat and hard work that I'd become so

familiar with from my training sessions, was now replaced by a musky foul stench that cloaked the basement. My senses cowered in displeasure, but I was too close to the point of no return. I continued; hands still placed out to the sides of me, now on the uneven surfaces of the bannisters framing the staircase.

At the same time my foot reached the bottom step, another feral noise pierced my ears and I blinked quickly, trying to adjust to the lights coming from around the corner.

What... The... Fuck.

Chapter Eighteen

THIS COULDN'T BE REAL. I had to be dreaming.

I took a step forward, allowing myself a better view of the tarpaulin that was rolled out across the length and width of the floor. A large metal table sat to the right-hand side of the room, parts of it worn with rust. I couldn't make out what was on top of it, Hank and Leonard stood in the way, skewing my examination of its contents.

My dad and two older brothers stood at the forefront of the chaos. My father's spine snapped to attention with what looked like a kitchen knife. He was further forward than Kian and Dax, creating a triangular form around what appeared to be someone curled up in a ball on the floor.

Wide-eyed, I scanned around the room, taking everything in. A glint of metal flickered under the light, drawing my attention to the knuckle dusters my brothers had placed on their hands, and I swear I saw blood dripping from them.

"You brought this upon yourself, you know if you'd just kept those dirty fucking hands away from those kids, then none of us would be here." The sinister tones of my dad's voice laced with pure fury sent chills up my spine, making the hairs on the back of my neck prick up on end. I'd never heard him sound like this. He was always so... *kind.*

Even if I wanted to, there was no way I could leave. My feet wouldn't move, and I was too curious to find out what the hell was going on.

Curiosity killed the cat, and all that.

I took a step towards my right, helping to conceal myself in the shadows and remain undetected. Calming my breath, I pinched my eyes tightly shut, praying that when I opened them, everything here would have just been some twisted sick nightmare.

It wasn't.

"You thought that going around touching little boys and girls was okay, did you?" Dax thundered through gritted teeth; his terrorising words cut into me like a knife.

Who was this man?

"It'll be impossible for you to do such a thing with no hands, won't it?" His threats scared me enough, and I wasn't the one in a heap on the floor. Yielding the knife above his head, my father swung it down into the man's arm which was sprawled out on the tarp, his hand now hanging on by a thread.

A literal fucking thread.

Screaming and thrashing himself around on the floor, my brothers looked down at him with total disregard to the pain the man was in.

"Here's how this is going to go. You're going to tell me who you're working for, how many more of you sick cunts there are, and where they are; and then maybe, just maybe, I'll let you walk out of here alive." Somehow, I felt like my father's words had no substance behind them, and although I would have never imagined him harming someone, the idea that he would let him walk free was almost impossible to comprehend.

It didn't take much for the man on the floor to start reeling off the information that my dad had ordered him to give up. Names and places started to fly at jet speed from his mouth. It was nothing like I'd ever seen before. I felt like I had walked into a scene of *The Godfather* minus the cigars and cannelloni.

Now out of breath, he lay there on the floor still gripping onto his hand and trying to regain control of his lungs. His secrets were out, as well as those of the people he'd just openly dropped in the shit with my father and brothers, and if this show was anything to go by, then they were all definitely, completely, one hundred percent, fucked.

I listened in as my father positioned himself just feet away from the man crying like a baby on the floor.

"Please, don't hurt me. I didn't mean to do what I did," he choked out between the snot dripping from his nose.

Weak.

"Y-You don't understand, they would have killed me. I swear I never touched them like the rest of them did."

My mouth was dry, my palms had started to clam up, and I could no longer feel my legs underneath me, and I wondered how I'd managed to stand up for so long.

"I don't give a fuck." Dax barked, stepping forward, rubbing his metal plated hand in the other. "You're a part of all of this. You think those kids wanted to be abducted? Do you think they wanted to be taken away from their parents? Do you think they wanted the hands of slimy old men put upon their little bodies? You're a fucking animal." Closing the gap between them, Dax lifted his hand above his head and planted a fist into his face, the metal making the most horrific crunch against the predators jaw.

"And do you know what happens to animals that can't be controlled?" He asked, waiting for an answer that never came. Instead, the man just lay there on the blood-stained tarp, holding his face, in defeat, with both of his hands. "I asked you a fucking question," he sneered - but still, no answer.

"I'll tell you what happens." Kian interjected, taking a stride in the direction of Dax and the bag of bloodied flesh and bones on the ground. "They get put down." This time, there was no impact from a metal plated knuckle, there was no sound from splitting flesh or broken teeth. Instead, there was complete silence.

I watched on, and part of me hoped that they would let him go, but the other part of me wanted him off of the streets and away from whatever heinous crimes he'd committed. Gathering from the conversational evidence, the guy being kept hostage by my family was not a nice man. He'd messed around with kids, and there was no excuse for that. No one had the right to take someone's innocence.

I could vouch for that.

Leonard slinked towards the table, finally allowing me a better view of the items my family had chosen to pack out their armoury with - a screwdriver, a metal pole, pliers, an axe. The list was endless, and I couldn't help wondering what on earth some of these things would have been used for, and I didn't know if I wanted to find out. Yet, I stayed in position, my hand on the wall steadying myself, hoping that my legs didn't buckle beneath me. I felt crazy for allowing myself to stay here and watch on as events unfolded, but curiosity got the better of me. I kept reminding myself that there was a reason my father and brothers were doing this.

He was a molester.

A child abuser.

A monster.

There was nothing in the world that made that acceptable.

My blood warmed underneath my skin, as I waited for what came next. I didn't know how this was going to end. Would they let him go like they had said they would? Or would he meet his end at the hands of the three men stood in front of him? Would they be the last faces that he would ever see?

Leonard grabbed hold of the shiny metal pole that lay perfectly placed on the table, and paced over to where my father stood, still in the same position, my brothers now both in front of him, glaring down at the predator on the floor.

Handing it over to my dad, Leonard turned on his heel and traipsed back next to Hank. A sinister grin painted his face, giving me the impression that this wasn't the first time he'd been involved in something like this. It seemed that this was something they'd done one too many times before.

With his head still drooped to the floor, his eyes flicked up and terror took over the man's face, the realisation had hit both him and I at the same time. They weren't going to let him go, no way. They were going to finish him and all of the sickening acts that he'd committed, and something told me that this was just the beginning of the clear out.

They had names, and places, times and numbers of people involved in these crimes, and after observing the things I had down in this hidden battle arena, my family wouldn't let this settle. They would do everything they could to stop these people. I knew what they stood for, and ultimately, I'd become a product of their morals. They wanted to help people in trouble. They had helped me, they'd pulled me, a child, out of a place that I couldn't rescue myself from and saved my life.

"You said you would let me go if I told you everything, a-and I have, you p-promised me that you'd let me walk." He begged, his voice trembling under every word. A sudden understanding hit him, and within that split second, he knew that my father's promises were empty.

They didn't mean shit.

"Let's be honest here, you're a dead man walking anyway. If we let you go, everyone in your organisation would know that it was you that had dobbed them in. You would have a target on your back even bigger than the one you had on your back when we found you." My father's words caused his head to drop, almost in agreement with what he'd said.

I didn't know how all of this stuff worked, but I'd seen enough films where the snitch gets roughed up or killed. This was inevitable. He wouldn't last five minutes, even if my dad did let him go. There would be no witness protection programme, there would be no fake passports enabling him to flee from England, there would be nowhere for him to go but back to the only life he knew. A life back with the people whose names he'd just willingly given to the three men who'd taken me in all those years ago. Three men who clearly had no issues with killing other people.

Oh, he was soooo fucking done for.

There was no doubt that somehow, the people that this person worked with would find out that he'd handed over information to stop their dealings. The dealings of poor innocent fucking kids.

My mind raced back to my school days and how I saw kids unable to save themselves at the hands of a bully... a school bully, someone the same age as them. I had to stop them. I remember it feeling so powerful, so good to have done something to protect them, to make their lives easier, to save them from the one thing they were scared of in life.

Without any form of warning, my legs suddenly walked me out of the darkness that I'd parked myself in for the last god knows how many minutes. Time seemed to move at a different rate down here. Like I was living in a different dimension, nothing seemed real. Reality had been flipped on its head and I was living in an alternate universe.

The sound of my own footsteps added more drama to the battle song of this war, a dire scene being played out in front of me. Spinning their heads in my direction, every single one of their attentions focused on me.

A look of hope filled the eyes of the man on the floor.

"Oh my God, p-please, you need to help me!" He screamed. "They're trying to kill me. Please save me." His words made me feel nothing. I thought they would, but they didn't. I didn't care. I didn't care that he'd been beaten to a pulp, or that he'd lost a few teeth during his stay at our country manor. All I could think of was those kids that he'd been involved with.

"Tanner, you shouldn't be here." My father muttered, looking over his shoulder at me. I knew that I shouldn't, this isn't something they would have wanted me to see, otherwise I would have been let down here before. I would have had a key to the basement, I would have been in on all of this. I would have been standing up there next to my brothers in camaraderie.

"You need to go. You don't want to see what's about to

happen. You need to leave." Dax said while walking over to me.

Trying to open my mouth to speak, I realised that the man on the floor was getting to his feet, my words failing me as everyone in the room turned their attention to focus solely on me. He was up and stumbling towards the table with the arsenal, his injured hand dangling around at his side.

Picking up something—anything—he raised it above his head and charged at my father.

"Dad!" I managed to shout, my voice finally coming back to life. He and my brothers turned on their heels, to see the predator heading towards our direction... Until, he wasn't.

A gun sounded off from the side of me. I jumped back as the noise pierced through my ears, but my eyes remained on him. Our eyes remained on each other. I held his gaze as he fell down to his knees, blood now leaking from his mouth, spluttering everywhere, as he flopped forward onto the floor, a bullet entry mark right between his eyes.

And it hit me.

I was the last face that he would ever see.

Chapter Nineteen

It had been two weeks since the bloodshed occurred in our basement. I was standing on the floorboards above a murder scene. I still didn't know how I felt about it. I knew what he'd done was wrong, but I couldn't get the look on his face out of my head. I watched on as his last bit of life left his body, and in that moment, I didn't feel a thing.

It wasn't the fact that he'd been killed that was making me feel uneasy, but the fact that I felt no remorse, which was the one thing that didn't sit well with me.

After everything that happened with Durham, I still felt some kind of guilt when I put him in the hospital. It was just who I was. Being at the forefront of his torture had a personal effect on my life, and even though I saw friends put in hospital because of the things he'd done, I still had a niggling doubt in the back of my mind about how the situation ended. I'd never been involved with the guy that had been killed in our basement, I didn't know him and I didn't give a fuck about him, but I felt that for some reason I should.

My brothers and father had spoken to me, they'd

explained everything, coming clean about everything they did. Things I had no idea about. Things that I didn't agree with. Murder, drugs, weapon importation. That's how my dad had made so much money, that's why I was able to live in this house, and go to a private school; that's why my dad had so much power in the city.

The only people they'd bring down to the basement were paedophiles, child abusers, people that prayed on the weak, I couldn't argue with that. Even though I'd never been sexually assaulted by anyone that my mum had brought into the house, I knew what it felt like to fall victim to those kinds of people. I had the scars to prove it, both mentally and physically.

In some weird way I knew that what they were doing was for the good of the city. It had come to my father's attention that there was a sex trafficking ring working in the outskirts of London, one of his friend's daughters had been a subject to the abuse and taken from a park near their home. Somehow, and luckily, they had managed to track down the person that had kidnapped her, that person being the one that I'd witnessed being shot between the eyes two weeks ago.

He told me that he needed to stop them, he needed to save as many children as possible from being snatched up. My dad had no idea how many kids had already gone missing, but checking the local crime statistics, it had become apparent that the number of kidnappings in our area had shot up by sixty-eight percent in the last six months - the highest that it had ever been. The rate of kidnappings was now more than the number of robberies, and for London, crimes of theft were always high, so they knew that it was a problem.

The drugs on the other hand, was something that I

couldn't get. I never would be able to understand, no matter how much my father explained their business plan to me, it was something that would never ever sit right in my chest. I'd seen my mother die because of her addiction. It had been me who had had to clear up her mess each time she'd go and get high. It had been me who'd been there to pick up the pieces of her broken soul when she'd tried to get clean, only for her to relapse and allow me to be exposed to it over and over again. I'd been the one to find her laying there dead with a fucking needle sticking out of her skin.

My dad appreciated this and he knew that it wasn't easy for me to comprehend, so after our initial conversation, he never brought up the drugs unless I asked about it. Over the last two weeks, I'd posed a number of questions to him; why drugs? Why help people to kill themselves? I just couldn't get a grip of why they would do it.

He explained that he started his shipment business before he'd had Dax and Kian, and that ultimately that had been where he'd made his money. He was London's biggest importer and exporter in a lot of things; fine wines and cars, everything the rich man could want. He was able to organise things so precisely that people trusted him to get their shipments in and out of the county without being detected. He was *good* at it.

I tried not to think about the drugs, and in my ignorance, I pushed it to the back of my mind, focusing on my father's more legal importations, and after a few days of interrogating my father and brothers about them, my focus changed to the predators that they got their hands on.

This was something that I wanted to be a part of. I wanted to help people, the same way that I'd helped the kids at Oakland Academy all of those years ago. The same way that I wanted to help Lily. I wanted to rescue people from all of the bad in their lives.

I vowed to be the person I needed when I was a kid, even if it meant tarnishing the walls with the blood of these predators. It was ironic that the place that once acted as my saviour, the place that my brother's had taught me to fight in, now stood as the ruin of scumbags like the one I witnessed receiving a bullet into his skull.

I wanted to hate myself for thinking this way, but as hard as I tried, I had no negative feelings towards this part of my dad's business. I wanted to help, I wanted to be included in this. I wanted to free the world of the people that caused harm to helpless victims.

And that's exactly what I planned on doing.

Chapter Twenty

"Dad, I want to do this." I argued with him. He thought I was too young to be part of the business.

"You need to focus on your studies, that's final." I knew that he wouldn't compromise on this with me, but I needed to explain to him why this was something that I had to be a part of.

"Dad, when you found me, you know those marks on my little body, they were caused by people like the ones you deal with. They were because I was subjected to abuse." I left it open to him to interpret the level of torture that I'd endured, wishing not to reveal any information that might lead him to tell me no again. "Those men, the ones my own mother had allowed to enter my life did those things to me. They took belts to my skin; they burned me with their cheap cigarettes. I know what it feels like to be in their position, and you're going to deny me helping them?" His face dropped, turning white under my admission.

I think it's worked, Tanner. I think you might have just won this battle.

"I'm sorry for everything you went through. You know I

am, but I just can't have my youngest son see the things we do."

"I don't know if you've forgotten, but I've already seen what you do dad! I've seen the weapons laid out on the table; I've seen a random guy get shot in the fucking head. I've seen the life drain out of someone that I didn't know as I looked him directly in the eye. I've seen the last look on someone's face before their lifeless body crashed onto the fucking plastic sheets underneath them. Please just let me do this."

I stood there in the doorway of the office I'd been in so many times, as my dad sat in the chair where he'd comforted me, where he'd listened about my school day, where he'd congratulated me on my grades and for making it onto a number of the sports teams. It felt surreal that I was now in that same room asking his permission to kill people.

"I don't want to be a part of anything else that you guys do, and you know why that is. I could walk out of here, and just try my hardest to forget everything that I saw that afternoon, to forget about the conversations we've had over the last month. But the truth is, every time I close my eyes at night, I can't help but think about those helpless kids that are out there, unable to do anything about the situation that they've been forced into."

Leaning back in his chair, my dad placed his palms together and closed his eyes, letting his head drop backwards, a tell-tale sign that he was doing some of his deep thinking. I'd exhausted every avenue with him, argued my case as though I was fighting for my freedom in a court of law. I had nothing left to give him. It was all over to him now. He was the judge, jury and executioner.

Releasing a sharp breath, I turned on my heels, and left the room. It would be no help if I was standing there waiting for him to decide. I knew him, he wouldn't jump to anything quickly, no matter how much pressure I put on him.

"You ready for this?" My brother asked as we stood in the basement of the house. Today, I would be facing my first official predator. I'd read the file on Ethan Jamison. I'd read every single fucking page ten times over.

I'd done all that my father had asked of me. I'd studied hard and finished all of my exams, passing in the top five percent of the school. Being academic came almost natural to me, and my love of history and books made it easier for me to knuckle down and get the grades I wanted.

I knew everything about this bastard. His date of birth, where he'd grown up, the fact that he had no brothers or sisters, which meant he was unable to prey on his own flesh and blood. Instead, he'd been part of the same ring of people who took other people's kids from parks and shopping centres, loading them into the backs of vans and taking them to remote locations across the country.

I had a list of the crimes that he'd committed both on and off the record. From petty theft, to breaking and entering when he was a teenager, to indecent exposure in his mid-twenties. He was now fifty-six years old. And he was a child molester.

When Hank and Leonard had caught up with him halfway up the country in Birmingham, he was found in the back of a black van with his hands on a nine-year-old boy. This information alone fuelled me enough to want to rip the cunts head off as soon as he was brought into the basement, but I'd been given strict instructions that nobody who came here was let off lightly.

They liked to toy with them, torture them and cause an excessive amount of pain on each and every single one of them before they killed them. Something sick and twisted inside me felt excited about getting my hands on him. He had a thing for young boys, according to his file, the younger the better. The rage that grew inside of me with every second I spent in the basement waiting for him was unbearable, and it took a crazy amount of control not to smash my fist into the wall.

"They're pulling in now. Get ready - and don't do anything *stupid*."

Chapter Twenty-One

He lay on the floor motionless.

He was dead.

Hank had checked to make sure of that. Something that I couldn't understand. During the time we'd been down here, he'd had his dick severed off, along with one of his hands. I had to commend them on the well thought out plan they'd concocted. It wasn't a quick death, but slow and painful. It was torturous and I won't deny that I loved every second of it.

A sense of freedom washed over me, it made me feel somewhat lighter, a small fragment of my suffering left me as his soul left him. Knowing that I'd been a part of stopping this person from hurting anybody else, provided me with an odd sense of comfort. He couldn't harm anyone ever again. Call it what you want, but that filled me with warmth and hope. We'd get these people and more some.

Looking at the blood that had been shed, I'm not going to lie and say that it didn't get to me, I'd thrown up three times already since he'd been down here. Now, I understood the need for the tarp across the room. It was insane how much blood there was in the human body. When you learn about it in science, the average number of pints doesn't sound like a lot, it's different when the crimson is poured out in front of you though. A sea of red covering the surrounding area glistened under the bright LED lights, and for a while I just stood there taking it all in, before chucking my guts up again.

My hands shook from the adrenaline that was pumping through my veins, as I traced my hand across a pair of pliers on the table in front of me. Reliving the image of how I used them. With Dax and Kian pinning Jamison down on the floor with the help of other restraints around his neck and legs, I'd attached them to his teeth, one by one, slowly pulling them from his gums. That was nothing in comparison to what he'd done to those kids – and nothing in comparison to what else had been done to him that night.

Walking away from the table, a broom handle sat propped against the wall. The bloody tip balancing on the floor, the crimson clotting up the shaft. Kian was a sadist when it came to torturing people—a professional, some might say—but knowing where that broom handle had been a couple of hours ago, made my stomach churn over. Well, now he knew what it felt like to have something invade his insides and cause damage like he'd done to those kids.

Rot in fucking hell.

Two Years Later

Chapter Twenty-Two

She hadn't been to school today—again—and honestly, I didn't know what more I could do. After threatening the new kid on so many occasions, it became clear that he had nothing to do with the change in Lily's emotional state. Although it did do some kind of good; it had put him in his place, and he'd calmed down a whole lot, which gave me some kind of pride knowing that I'd sabotaged another potential threat to the students at Oakland.

Her behaviour over the last month or so had altered drastically. She wasn't acting like the girl she once was, and on the odd chance that I did get to see her, she didn't even look like the old Lily. She was completely unrecognisable; she'd lost a crazy amount of weight, making her already tiny stature now pretty much non-existent. The dark circles surrounding her eyes had become a permanent feature on her pale face, her eyes had sunk into her head, her cheekbones protruding even more than they ever had done, and her hair had thinned out. Even when we were younger, she'd always made sure that she looked nice, she was a firecracker, and I remember the countless arguments that her and my aunt would get into because Lily didn't like the dress that had been chosen out for her to wear. She had her own unique style, she didn't give a shit about what other people thought and I think that was one of her best traits.

My uncle had died last year, and I know that this had probably played a part in the decline of Lily's health even more than before. They'd been so close, the best of friends, and growing up I was lucky enough to have been part of his life. He loved me like I was his own, that was the thing about this family, everyone looked out for each other, everyone was an equal, there was nothing that could be done to break up this unit. The bond we had was an unwritten oath, if you were in this family, then you were in it for good, through everything that happened, the good and the bad.

Making my way through the front door of my aunt's house, I found her sitting in the kitchen, a cup of tea in hand, steam coming from the top. Taking a sip from the white China cup, she looked over, giving me a helpless half-hearted smile. I always joked with her, saying that she had a mouth made of asbestos, she could drink tea straight from the pot without it burning. Even now, I added cold water to my coffee so it was drinkable.

This time, I didn't make the joke, instead, I dragged myself over to where she sat on the kitchen chair, and placed my arms around her, pulling her frail body into a hug, careful not to break her. The last year had taken a huge toll on her health too, and we were all busy trying to rescue the both of them.

"I miss him, Tanner." She sobbed into my shoulder. I had to take a moment to try and swallow down the lump forming in my throat before replying.

"I know. I miss him too." There was so much more I

wanted to say, but I was frightened of breaking down in front of her, and God knows I needed to be strong for her and Lily.

"I miss Lily too."

I miss her too.

Her words cut so deep into me, that I could feel them attacking every inch of my skin. It seemed that she'd already come to terms with the loss of someone who was still alive and breathing in one of the rooms upstairs, which made this whole situation worse.

"You know that Leonard's leaving?" Of course I did, but I knew my aunt was making conversation with me.

"Yeah, I know. Said something about having cancer and wanting to spend the time he had left with his parents." As much as I didn't like Leonard, his story hit close to home, most likely because my uncle had gotten cancer and died.

Blinking the ever-growing tears away, I hugged her tighter, letting her know that I was there for her without saying a word. Composing myself, I eventually released her. Not that I wanted to, but I needed to go in and check on Lily. I had two people in this house who relied on me now, and there was no way in hell that I was going to let either of them down.

"I'll go and see Lily, and then I'll be back. She's going to be alright. Okay?" My words were soft, providing her with the reassurance that she most definitely needed. Truth was, I couldn't guarantee that she would be. Lily had hardly spoken recently, so finding out what it was that was wrong was becoming more and more impossible with every waking day. The chance of helping her out of this hole she had found herself in, was becoming less likely to happen, and I hated myself for not being able to do something.

Stood outside of the door to Lily's bedroom I braced myself for what was on the other side before knocking. I don't know why I bothered, she never gave me the go ahead to come in, she probably knew that I would regardless.

Sat in her chair by the window, the usual spot she was always in, she didn't acknowledge me, something she'd gradually stopped doing over time. Long gone were the days that she'd greet me with a big grin on her face and a massive hug. That was over, I was lucky enough if I got her to look at me nowadays. She just stared out the window, a vacant look in those troubled eyes of her.

It killed me to see her like this. I just wanted to sweep her up and take her away from whatever it was that was causing her so much pain, but honestly, I don't even think that would help. She was too far gone, she was beyond repairing. We just had to ride out whatever this was and pray to the fucking gods above that she would get better.

"I miss you Lil," I whispered as I took a perch on the windowsill opposite to her chair. Looking out onto the fields at the back of the property, I wondered for a moment what she was thinking of. Did she want me to carry on visiting her? Did she want to be left alone? Was I fighting a losing battle?

We sat there in silence, taking in the sunset that was fast approaching in the sky. The distance fading out, just like Lily was. If this was the only interaction that I got with her, then I was happy with that, it was enough for me. As long as she knew that I was there for her, even if she didn't want to share anything with me, then I was doing my job. I would never walk away from her; we didn't walk away from one another in this family.

"I miss you too."

Tipping my head towards the last of the sun and closing my eyes, I struggled to get a handle on my emotions. My breath hitched, and the tears that I'd fought back for so long began to stream down my face. Still, I kept my head firmly facing the window. Hearing Lily's voice for the first time in what felt like a lifetime had sent me over the edge. It wasn't the voice I was so used to hearing, and instead of the cheerful vibrations of her words drilling through my ears, it was the complete opposite. The hoarse tones of her sombre voice was now filled with darkness.

She'd spoken to me. After all this time, she'd finally spoken. I couldn't help but become hopeful that this was a breakthrough, and that maybe, just maybe we might have turned a corner.

I prayed that tomorrow, the new dawn of day would bring back another little piece of the Lily I knew.

Chapter Twenty-Three

Lily

To my dearest mother,

I don't know where to start, but I know where this is going to end.

I've tried, I've tried so hard mummy, but I can't take this anymore. I can't take the torturous pain. It's become too much for my little shoulders to carry, I've tried to bear the weight as best I can, the heaviness of letting what's been happening, happen to me. I don't know who I am anymore, and I'm so consumed by the thoughts in my mind, and I don't know how to deal with it – thoughts that someone my age shouldn't have to struggle with. It feels like I'm walking around with concrete blocks attached to every single one of my limbs, and no matter how hard I try to break out of them, they will always have a hold on me.

He will always have a hold on me.

I wish that I could have spoken to you about

what I was going through. I wish I could have told you, or one of the boys at least, what was happening to me. I know you would have been able to help me - God knows you would have done everything in your power to. I know my cousins would have fought to the death for me, the same way that daddy would have if he was still with us.

The truth is, I'm ashamed that I let it happen to me, that I let him put his hands on me, that I let him take my innocence from me. It's being going on for a while; four years, seven months and twenty-nine days now to be exact.

I often wondered what it would feel like to not have to wake up every day knowing that my 'protection' would be the complete opposite and hurt me instead. I know he's not here anymore, I heard that he's left, but that doesn't get rid of everything that I'm feeling.

I'm so messed up and the demons in my head won't leave me alone. I'm too tired to fight against them anymore, I can't see a way out of this. There isn't anything on this planet that could release the chains that they have wrapped around my heart.

Most days I can't even open my eyes at the fear of what might happen, of how I might feel. I either feel everything at once, or nothing at all. And I can't live another minute like that.

I was looking out of the window this afternoon, the sun was shining on the flowers, and I could see Tanner and Kian playing football with one another on the lawns, and I knew they were here to look after us mummy. Knowing that you have them in your life, made me feel – for the first time, in a long time – somewhat okay. I know they worry about me, and I know they make sure they take time out of their busy lives to come and see me, but I don't want to be a burden to any of you anymore.

Knowing that there is a way that I can take away the fact that I tarnish your days with my depression and torment makes my heart feel at ease. The clouds that once roamed my war-stricken mind suddenly began to lift, and everything seemed clearer. I understand what it is that needs to be done to free myself from it - from him - completely.

I wrote you this letter to tell you how much I love you, and how you were, are, and always will be my everything. I'm looking at a picture of us, the one from my eleventh birthday party - you know the picture I mean, the one where I'm wearing the pretty dress we'd picked out together especially for the party. We all look so happy. This is what I want to remember, this is the last thing that I will look at before I meet my final destination. I'm burning the image into my head, so that I never forget it, so that I never forget you all.

Please know that this isn't your fault, not yours, not Uncle G's, not the boys, but you have to understand that the ache in my heart is making it impossible to get any peace, and I need peace more than anything in the world. I need to rest now mummy. I need to be at peace, and I can only do that if I'm not here, I can't do it feeling the way that I do inside.

I know you'll cry, and I know you'll miss me, and that's okay, but promise me that you won't question yourself. This world has been amazing and beautiful, but it has also been so evil and cruel and unkind to me.

I need to go now. I need to be with daddy.

Until we meet again someday, always know that I love you and I'll miss you.

Lily.

Chapter Twenty-Four

Fuck.

Fuck. Fuck. Fuck.

I held the letter to my chest, trying to process everything that I'd just read whilst my heart shattered into a million tiny pieces onto the floor beneath me.

She was gone.

She was really fucking gone.

The crimson water-stained photograph of our family, that was sat on top of Lily's suicide note on my father's desk, proved that. I pulled the letter away from my chest, lessening the beating of my heart which was smashing violently against my ribs, in a mix of anger and hopelessness, and read it again.

And again.

And again.

Slumping myself against the bookcase of the office, I didn't know if I would ever recover from this. She was like a sister to me, we'd known each other for so long now, we'd been through so fucking much. I know I had my brothers, but there was a bond between Lily and I that could never be broken, nothing could or would ever come between us.

I stared down at the letter, the seconds ticking over into minutes. I couldn't understand any of this.

How did we not know?

How the hell didn't a single one of us fucking know?

Walking back to the desk and shakily placing the note back in its envelope addressed to my aunt.

'It's not your fault... not the boys... I need to go now...'

Leonard had cancerously injected himself into my baby cousin's life and taken everything from her; her innocence, her ability to be happy and her life. He'd taken it all, every single damn thing, and then fucked off leaving nothing but a fucking suicide note in her wake, a suicide note he'd basically coerced Lily into writing.

He'd made her feel like there was nothing else left in this world for her. She had everything. She had us. And yet he'd still managed to twist her mind so much that she didn't think that her life was worth living anymore. To me, there is no crime worse than that, nothing in this world could be worse than making someone feel as though they can't go on in this world a minute longer because of the cruel and inexplicable things they'd done to them.

He was going to fucking pay.

An eye for a fucking eye.

Clenching my fists tightly, I rammed it into the naked brick wall that housed a fireplace sitting adjacent to the window and let out an indignant roar as my knuckles split open on impact. I'd lost my head and apparently my pain threshold had disappeared too, my pain receptors completely dissolved, with no awareness of the agony that should be radiating in my hand.

I hit the wall with my other hand, this time harder.

And again, this time leaving blood on the walls.

I didn't care how much it should be hurting; nothing would ever compare to the pain Lily had endured at the hands of Leonard. The fact she'd taken a blade down her wrist, without a second thought, authenticated the trauma that monster had left her in.

She had time to decide not to do it, she'd written a letter, inking out all of her feelings, and that still wasn't enough time to make her realise that she didn't have to do it. She really didn't want to be here. Her fate was sealed way before she picked up the pen to write the letter.

Rage continued to build up inside of me, and this time, no matter how hard I tried to coax myself down from the self-destructive ledge that I'd found myself teetering on so many times before, nothing would work – not until I'd avenged her.

Turning on my heels and pacing around the oblong oak conference table towards the safe that was meticulously hidden behind an expensive large cream and gold abstract painting, I pulled it off the wall before punching in the code and swinging the door open. Standing back, I rested both hands on the metal frame of the safe, breathing wildly and trying to steady myself.

I'd experienced enough loss to never need another lesson in heartbreak again, but this had fucked me one hundred and fifty percent. Grabbing the Glock 19 from the safe, I knew that I had the power to stop another helpless child from experiencing the damage and distress that Lily felt at the hands of *him*. I made a vow to myself that I would find the bastard that did this and make him pay, he would never rip the innocence or take the future away from someone again.

Rushing out of the office, weapon in hand and an

armour of anger weighted on my shoulders, I slammed the door open, nearly losing it off the hinges, almost as much as I'd lost my temper.

"We can't find him," Dax admitted, as I came face to face with him in the doorway.

"I will." I hissed. "I'll find him, and when I do, I'm going to make that motherfucker pay for everything he's put this family through."

"Brother, trust me when I say that we've exhausted every avenue trying to find him. He's off the radar. He knows how to play us. He was one of *us*." Those five words churned my stomach, nearly as much as reading Lily's note did, I hadn't seen my father since he'd locked himself away three days ago, since my aunt had found Lily's body in the fucking bathtub, a family photo lying next to her, dropped out of her lifeless grip and a goddamn suicide note on the vanity table in her bedroom.

I felt like my heart had been ripped clean out of my chest, the air sucked from my lungs and the prospect of finding Leonard slowly seemed to dwindle into the darkness. I knew full well that Dax would have taken lead whilst my father processed and tried to come to terms with what had happened to Lily.

Without doubt he'd be sitting in his room beating himself up about assigning Leonard to look out for her, only for it to be the worst decision he'd ever made, and trust me, my father had made a lot of bad decisions in his life; some of which he could have avoided and others whereby nothing he could have done would have changed the outcome. When it came to the subject of Lily, this was something that none of us could have predicted.

Chapter Twenty-Five

I NEEDED THIS TODAY. I needed to take out this fucking pain and anger on someone. It's been a whole week since Lily died. And for each of those days, I'd roamed the streets of London trying to find the person who had betrayed us the most. The cunt who had taken my little cousin away from us. I would find him, and when I did, he would regret everything he'd done to this family.

I would make him pay.

Waiting for the next delivery of trash to turn up, I paced the floor of the basement I'd stood in so many times before. Not that I found it difficult, but each time I was down here, the easier it was to end the life of someone, and today would be no exception. Again, I'd read the file, memorised what they'd done and imbedded every small detail into my brain. Today, this person would take the place of Leonard, and he would get everything I had in me and more.

I'd take no prisoners...

WASHING my hands of the blood from the last vigilante attack, I scrubbed them raw. Somehow, I felt like I had Lily's blood on my hands. I couldn't count the number of times that I'd read her note, nor the number of times I'd had this overpowering sense of guilt hanging over my head.

I miss you too.

Her final words played over and over like a broken fucking record in my head, but I needed to focus, I needed to find him. I didn't know how, but I would. I'd taken on Brandon to help me, he'd been with me over the last week, making sure that everyone was okay. I know that what happened to Lily had affected him as well, we'd been so close before all of this shit.

His dad had recently died, another trauma to add to the growing list of deaths that surrounded us, and I know that it had hit Brandon pretty hard. So as a family we'd helped make sure that he and his mum had everything they wanted and needed.

To say my dad was devastated was the understatement of the year, and he had given Brandon a job with us; probably not the type of job his mum had in mind for her son, but it was well paid, and like I said, we never turn our back on family.

"Bro, you need to slow down, you're going to run yourself into the ground." As much as Brandon was right, I didn't give him the satisfaction of agreeing with him. I was tired, so fucking tired, but in comparison to what Lily had been through it was nothing. The least I could do was find the bastard who did this.

Storming past Brandon in the kitchen, I ran upstairs to change into something more comfortable and grab a baseball cap. I never searched for Leonard as myself, he would spot me a mile off, being six-foot-four with auburn hair wasn't something that would go undetected to the majority of people. At least with a hat on my head, I felt somewhat inconspicuous moving through the busy streets of London.

Making my way down the stairs and towards the front door, Brandon threw his arm out in front of me.

"Move. Now."

"Dude, think about this. You know I want to help you, but it's been a week now, and even you dad's trained professionals can't find him. They've done everything, searched every bit of video footage from the street cameras and there's no trace of any calls being made to or from his phone, its off, and probably chucked in the Thames somewhere so it can't be traced." He rambled on, vocalising everything that I knew already. Listing everything that deemed it impossible to find the one person I wanted to get to the most.

"You've got to just trust him. Your dad knows what he's doing. They'll find him, and when they do, that's when you can kill the bastard, for us all." I let his words sink in. He was right. I knew he was right all along, but I just needed to feel like I was doing something, anything.

"Fine," I said, turning on my heel and stalking back up the stairs. I'll just dream of the day I get my hands on him.

Entering my bedroom in the left wing of the house, I picked up a photograph sitting on the side of my dresser, a picture of me and Lily that was taken just after she'd come first place in one of her dance competitions. Before everything went wrong. Before I started doing what I now do, before she killed herself. Back when everything was perfect. We were so young and unaware of what life would throw at us. Tears started to fill my eyes, but instead of blinking them away, I let them flow. The river of salty teardrops crashing on the parquet flooring of my room.

She deserved these tears.

Every single one of them.

Twelve Years Later

Chapter Twenty-Six

Arriving back after a month of being away, Grace welcomed me back into the family home.

"It's so good to have you back!" She chimed. I loved Grace, she'd always been like a mother figure to me, feeding me up well, and making sure she did all the maternal duties. She'd even taken it upon herself to give me the *birds and the bees* talk when she caught me in my bedroom with a girl from college. I still don't think I'll ever live that shame and embarrassment down.

I offered her a smile, reaching out my arm to touch her. It had been over a decade since we lost Lily, but I knew from Grace that you never truly get over things, we just learn to live with the sadness and grief and learn to live our lives without the people we'd lost.

Her daughter had died around the same time that I'd been found that day in the park. She'd never told me how, and I was clever enough not to ask too many questions. It turns out the teddy bear that she'd given me when I arrived home with the Lawsons, was her girl's.

It's nice to have her around, she makes me feel like my chaotic life is a bit more normal than it really is. Among all of the madness, Grace brings me a sense of calm, and on days like today that's exactly what I needed.

I'd been up north for the last month finalising some paperwork on one of my businesses. Since Lil died, I'd made it my own mission to celebrate her life and legacy in my own way.

Kian on the other hand, went through an obsessive phase trying to find Leonard, so much so, that he'd been caught by our father with a number of people in the boot of his car that he thought might be linked with his Houdini worthy disappearance. Obviously, they all ended up being dead ends. I think he was just out for blood - any blood.

After coming to terms with Lily's death and her funeral, I made a promise that I'd make something of myself, so that's what I did. I worked hard, creating business plans and propositions, finally coming up with my first business venture. *LL's Boxing*.

I wanted to do something for the community we lived in. Boxing had given me so much confidence and allowed me to stand up for myself and others. In a way, it saved me. So, I started renting a little run-down space in the centre of the city.

I remember opening day, the amount of support that I'd gotten from my family and the community was incredible. The gym had, and always will, provide a free safe haven for kids, whether they're in trouble or they need somewhere safe to be. I hired some trainers to teach the kids self-defence, and when we managed to get a bigger space, I installed a games room for them all to play in too.

I wanted to protect people. Always have, and always

will. It's something I couldn't do myself at one point in my life, and something I couldn't do for Lily no matter how hard I tried, and I think that over time, as the years have gone on, I realised that it wasn't any of our faults. It was *his*. He was to blame. All I could do now was channel my pain and sorrow into something more than he will ever be. He hadn't won.

Over the years I'd secured another two businesses, aside from LL's Boxing, I also had Lil's Florist and Lil's Kitchen, both of which now had branches in London and up north. Her legacy was spreading, and I knew that she'd be proud of me. I knew that if she were still alive, she'd have been bugging me to do the catering for her twenty-first birthday, and her wedding.

She was like that.

Even after everything that I'd been through, things were starting to look up, we were all even closer than we were before, it's crazy how something so harrowing can lead to something so beautiful.

My mum and Lily might be gone, but through it all, I'd been given the chance to be part of something incredible, and it was all thanks to my father. Without him, I wouldn't be here, I wouldn't have been given the opportunities that I'd had.

I wouldn't have been anything other than the son of a drug addict, who'd been found dead on a bench. I could imagine what the headlines in the local newspapers would have been. Would I have made the national news? Would I have had people from the community crying over my story if it had ended up different to how it did?

"Grace, where's dad? Have you seen him today?" I asked, expecting him to be in his office sorting some kind of business out like usual.

"He's gone for a walk; he should be back soon darling." She said as she scurried off into the kitchen. "Now what would you like to eat? You must be starving after that drive."

Chapter Twenty-Seven

I dropped the phone, smashing it into smithereens on the hard tiled floor.

I'm sorry to tell you, but your father, Garrett Lawson has been involved in an accident.

The doctors words spun in my head.

You need to get to St Thomas' as fast as you can.

How much more of this shit did life want to throw at me?

Chucking my coat on, I ran out of the door and got into my car, the smell of new leather seats hitting the back of my throat. Switching on the engine I waited for the car to warm up before I put it into gear. As much as I wanted to bomb it down the long gravel driveway, I remember my dad always telling me to let it tick over for a while before chucking it into gear, it was bad for the car if you didn't.

It's funny the things you remember in times like these.

My mind raced, presenting me with the worst-case scenario, that my father would be dead when I got there. That the last memory I would have of him, would be him asleep in his office chair, the day I left to go away on business.

I wanted more time with him. I'd already lost my mum and Lily; I couldn't lose my dad as well.

I owed him my life.

Pulling into the hospital I parked the car in the first parking spot I saw and rushed towards the accident and emergency apartment. He'd been out for his daily walk, something he'd been doing for the last twelve years – since we lost Lily.

He said he needed to start keeping fit, but my dad didn't walk anywhere, so deep down I knew that this was something he'd started doing to subside any thoughts and guilt he had about Lily's death. Almost as a way to clear his head and help him feel just that slight bit better.

In the days after her death no one had spoken to him. He wanted to be left alone, he wanted us nowhere near him, and we obeyed his orders, giving him the time and space that he so desperately needed. Now, whatever situation I found beyond those doors at the hospital, there was no way in hell that I would be leaving him. I would be by his side, making sure that he knew I was there for him.

I paced endlessly around the patient waiting room just outside of the entrance to the surgery suite, my brothers would be here soon, all I could do was sit tight. I'd not been given much information over the phone, other than that he'd been involved in a road traffic collision.

He wasn't in the car.

He was a pedestrian.

This made my stomach drop, the thought of him not being surrounded by the safety of the metal cage he'd usually be in meant that the damage to him was more than likely a lot more extreme than that of the driver. Although, as things came to light, the driver couldn't be found anywhere. They had fled the scene.

They'd left my dad for dead on the side of the road. They didn't stop to help him. And God knows that if my dad had caused someone harm—someone that didn't deserve it—he would have stayed and waited with them, making sure that he didn't leave until help had got to them. He would have held their hand and cared for them, because all of his bad things aside, he was a good man, he had a heart of gold, and there was nothing or no one on this planet that could take that away from him.

"Mr. Lawson?" A soft voice filled my ears, as a gentle hand was placed on my shoulder, stirring me from the sleep I must have drifted into whilst waiting for the doctors to update me on my father.

I looked around the waiting area, my brothers had arrived whilst I'd been passed out on one of the uncomfortable hospital chairs; you'd think considering the amount of time people spent waiting in these seats that they'd maybe get the funding for some that didn't make you feel like you needed a new spine.

"Yes, that's me..." I coughed, clearing my throat, trying desperately to lubricate it enough to carry on speaking. I stood up, the blood rushing to my head, dizziness taking over me. I needed something to eat, my stomach growled at me in protest as I tried to gather up some energy to hear what the docs were about to say.

Two exhausted looking doctors stood in the waiting room, their hair scruffy and darkened circles filled the space underneath their eyes. I knew on arrival that my dad had been rushed down for emergency surgery. There wasn't any time to for me to speak to or see him, no matter how much I wanted to.

"Doc, what's the situation?" Dax said, breaking the deadly silence that took over the waiting area. I'd only ever seen scenes like this in films, and we all know that there's only two ways that a something like this could end - life, or death.

The doctor looked at all three of us, and I knew that it wasn't good news. Just from the expression in their eyes, I knew that what they were about to say wasn't going to be the news that we all longed to hear.

"I'm sorry to tell you, but your father didn't make it." The surgeon placed a hand on Dax's shoulder, offering his condolences. I'd suffered enough loss in my life to know that a gentle touch wasn't going to cure the feeling that was revving up in my gut.

"We did everything we could, but unfortunately he'd suffered such a severe brain trauma, and extensive internal bleeding that we were unable to save him." The second doctor described. Kian threw his fist into the adjacent wall, letting out a deep gut-wrenching howl, leaving a hole in the dry wall.

Dax threw himself round, grabbing onto Kian by the waist, stopping him from doing any further damage to the hospital's interior, and I watched on as they both fell to the floor under buckled knees. It was as though I was experiencing an outer body experience, I wasn't there, it was just Dax and Kian who had lost a father. I got it, I knew that I wasn't their flesh and blood, but something deep down felt ignored in this situation.

"Thanks for letting us know." I nodded my head in their direction, and turned on my heels, allowing the tears in my eyes to stream down my face. How the hell do doctors do this day in and day out. It takes a superhero to stay so composed when offering such terrible news to the families of dead loved ones.

As I made my way towards the exit, hoping that some fresh air would tend to the wounds that sliced my heart open yet again, I questioned everything that I could have done differently. I could have stayed with my father; I didn't have to go away for work and leave him on his own. Why did he have to start walking? I didn't get it. Hank should have stopped him. I should have stopped him.

My father was dead. Another tragedy to add to my life that was already filled with so much suffering and grief.

"Where are you going?" Kian chased after me down the corridor towards the exit.

"I need to get out of here." I managed to choke out. My chest felt heavy and the suffocating feeling suddenly took over, I couldn't breathe. I needed to focus and get my shit together, and even though I wasn't their blood brother, I needed to get myself in the right mindset to look after the remaining members of my family. We had all lost someone today, but ultimately, they had lost the one person that had been with them since the day they were born. Since the day they had lost their mother all of those years ago.

"Stay with us." His voice cracked under the order. "We all need each other."

"I thought you might need some time with each other, you know, to process this." I said honestly.

"You have lost a father today as well. Don't ever forget that we are your brothers. We will always be brothers." Kian's words hit me round the back of the head like a metal pole, giving me the shake-up, I needed. They didn't see me as anything other than their brother, and even in this sad moment, my heart filled just a little bit with warmth. They wanted me to be with them, they saw me as an equal.

I don't know why I doubted it, but I guess part of me didn't know whether our dad was the one thing that was keeping us together. I didn't know if once we'd found out that he was dead, then they would slowly fade me out of their lives.

"Wait for us, and we'll come with you. We need to stick together. We're the only ones left now." Dax said stepping forward towards the spot that we stood in.

"Let me phone Hank," Kian rummaged in his pocket and pulled out his phone. Looking down at the screen, he hesitated before looking back up at us.

"No, I drove here, I'll take us home. We should wait until we get home before we tell him."

This would hurt Hank. More than anything.

Chapter Twenty-Eight

WE WERE ALREADY on the case to finding out who it was that had killed my dad. Hank had pulled himself together pretty damn quick when my brothers mentioned locating the person responsible. He'd gone from zero to one hundred real fast and started taking the necessary steps in order to get our hands on the scumbag.

Within a short amount of time, we'd managed to get hold of some CCTV footage from the surrounding areas of where the accident happened. My dad's contacts had sent us over a cut down version of the footage, starting from the street next to the crash site. As much as we wanted to find this person, we didn't want to see our father being thrown in the air like a ragdoll. Knowing that he wasn't with us anymore hurt enough.

Sitting in front of the large television placed on the wall of one of the rooms back at our house, we scanned through the footage, hoping for something to give us some information on who the culprit might have been. We'd managed to track down a man who looked to be in his mid-fifties and drunk. Stumbling down the streets, he made his way into a dive bar, somewhere that no one sitting in this room would have ever visited. As a family, we were more Royal Brackla Scotch as opposed to pints of Stella, dirty peanut dishes and wife beater shirts.

The video ended; we'd watched all of the footage we could get our hands on for the time being. Looking over at everyone else sat in the room, we all looked defeated and hopeless, except for Hank, who seemed as though he'd had a lightbulb moment. If we were in a cartoon, he'd have a big old shiny bright bulb floating over his head.

"I know that bar." Hank said grabbing his jacket that he'd flung over the arm of one of the luxury sofas housed in the cream and burgundy room.

"W-wait, where are you going?" I asked, before he charged out of the room.

"Look at the timestamp on the video, he could still be there. I'm going." Before any of us could stop him, he'd fled into the hallway and out of the front door, the engine to the Range Rover buzzed though my ears as he took off down the driveway.

He was right, there was the possibility that this man could still be at the bar, or at least somewhere close. The only problem was that it would take Hank a good twenty minutes to get into the city before he could start hunting this motherfucker down.

Chapter Twenty-Nine

Hank

Something told me that I was going to find him today, and deep in my bones, I knew that I wasn't going to return back to the house until I'd gotten my hands on him. I would avenge my best friend, no matter how long it took me. His three sons had lost their mothers, uncle, youngest cousin and now their father. This person wasn't going to get off lightly. He would pay for what he had done.

Chasing up the streets and into the city, I didn't have a game plan, but I knew I couldn't act on impulse, what I wanted to do to him would end up with me being arrested, and I couldn't add that onto the list of shit that the three boys had to deal with. I knew that they would also want a hand in his ending. I needed to keep level-headed, no matter how much I wanted to put a bullet into his skull.

Creating a plan in my head on the drive, the car moved sleekly along the roads, as the sun started to disappear slowly behind the city's skyline. Firstly, I needed to locate him, then I'd follow him until he ended up back wherever he lived. I'd need to get some background information on him, so I would need to call Troy up, the head of

Intelligence; he was the guy who would track down and provide the Lawsons with all the details of the predators we go after. He was a mastermind, with hacking skills that were a second nature to him. He was able to get into any database anywhere in the world and get hold of everything that we might need to do our job. When we had drug shipments coming in and out of London, he was the one who could alter the CCTV cameras that would lead to the most undetected of operations. Garrett had a lot of contacts that he'd built relationships with over the years, all of whom he'd entrusted me to manage.

Pulling up outside of the bar from the footage, I put the handbrake on and stepped out of the car, making my way towards the entrance sliding my hands into the leather gloves that I'd thrown in the car and onto the passenger seat. For some reason, wearing gloves made me feel just that little bit less uneasy about being caught in my line of work.

I pushed open the dilapidated wooden door, and a bell rang above my head as I stepped over the threshold and into the confines of a dark dingey room. The smell of cheap whiskey invaded my nose, causing the back of my throat to itch, and I thanked the heavens above, that I wasn't used to being in a place like this, that I was fortunate enough to have the life I had, and to have had the best friend that I did.

All three of the boys reminded me of him so much, I knew that once this was over, I might find it difficult to look at them without being reminded of my dear friend, but we were all we had now, they were my only family, and I loved all three of those boys as if they were my own. Each of their stories had a special place in my heart, which made me love them even more.

Especially Tanner.

This family, as a collective, had seen more death than

one could imagine. Were the deaths of their family members being passed on as revenge for all the harm and suffering that we'd inflicted on the monsters we dealt with on a weekly basis? Was this our karma - to have everyone we loved die?

I tried hard to shake the thought from my mind as I scanned around the bar, hoping to catch a glimpse of the man who'd killed Garrett, but he was nowhere to be seen.

I needed a drink.

Perching myself on a stool near the entrance of the bar door, I waited for the bartender to take my order. A scotch on the rocks, but that of the petrol kind – I doubt they served any of the good stuff we had back at the house. I winched as I tried to swallow down the brown liquid from the glass he'd just rinsed under the tap, and prayed to God that I didn't catch something from drinking out of it.

"Can I get you another?" The bartender asked me, flashing me a grin, showing a gap from a missing tooth, just like the one Leonard had.

Damn I wished we'd caught that fucker.

Raising my hand and giving him the thumbs up to order another drink, I noticed some commotion at the back of the bar over by a sign to the toilets. My natural instinct was to stand up and make my way over to the trouble; this was something that had been embedded in me. Trouble seemed to follow me everywhere, and each time I'd rise to the challenge of ending it, even if I got hurt in the process. I'd gotten much better at dealing with trouble now compared to when Garrett and I first met, I couldn't throw a punch to save my life, which seemed funny to Garrett considering I was a lot bigger than him, and he could have easily knocked me out in one or two throws. Instead, I sat tight on the rickety barstool and flicked my eyes over the men by the toilets. He was here.

Picking up the glass of whatever it was that I'd been served, my focus remained fixed on him as he made his way towards where I was sitting by the door of the bar. He was awkward on his feet, representing a new-born foal, he was all over the place and it was embarrassing to see an old man in such a state. I don't even think I recall seeing the boys like that when I'd picked them up from parties and nightclubs when they were teenagers.

I almost felt sorry for the guy in front of me, who knows what kind of life he'd had. Had something happened to him to make him this way? I let my mind trail off, before giving myself a kick up the ass and getting back to business. I couldn't let the notions that something may have caused this behaviour make me lose my focus on the task at hand.

Throwing back the contents of the glass and chucking a twenty down on the side of the bar, I picked up the keys to the car and slowly started to follow him, turning the opposite direction to where he was heading to get back to the car. I could have taken all day, by the time I'd slid into the driver's seat, started the car, and started pulling away onto the side road, he'd only managed to make it about one hundred yards down the street, knocking into walls as he went.

We were on the outskirts of the city, so following him in a car became a bit obvious as the traffic dwindled down. I needed to do this on foot to go unnoticed. Indicating into a car park to the right of me, I pulled into a space and jogged towards the pay and display meter—no way I'm getting clamped today—I'd made that mistake in the heat of the moment one too many times before.

Putting the ticket on the dashboard of the car, I

slammed the door shut and sprinted towards a hole in the metal wire fence, I'd seen the man stumble down the side alley. I had no idea where he was going, and no idea who he would meet when he got there, but I pushed forward, following behind him careful not to draw attention to myself. I could be putting myself in potential danger here, no one knew where I was, and I had no idea what kind of person I was dealing with.

Taking a number of turns down through housing estates and further out onto the edge of the city, we ended up by a marshland, trees and wildflowers blanketing the floors below my feet and skies above us. Turning down an unmade path, a house became visible, something which you wouldn't have put in the boroughs of London.

Although the house was run down, you could tell just by looking at the building that, once upon a time, it was probably a beautiful home to someone. The structure appeared hand crafted, the details on the eaves, carved to perfection. It seemed sad to think that someone had abandoned the upkeep of the property.

I stood in the shadows of the trees and watched over, waiting to see what Garrett's killer did next. Taking something out of his pocket, I reached for the gun that sat in the holster under my jacket, preparing myself to use it if I needed to. Taking out a key and clumsily sauntering through the off-white picket fence that surrounded the property, he made it to the door without falling flat on his face.

He could barely walk, let alone drive a car. I wondered if the vehicle had been found yet. We'd been so focused on finding the man who had hit Garrett, that we forgot to consider the possibility of tracing the car down, something that might have given us more information on who the perpetrator might have been. This is why this family needed Garrett, he was always full of logical ideas, and his thought process always served the best possible route of execution.

This was the man's house.

Picking out my phone from my pocket, I scrolled through the phone list, and pulled up Troy's number and hit dial.

"Troy." I whispered. "I need you to pull up some info on a property for me. I'll send you my location, you'll see it on there, it's the only house in the area. Text me over the details when you get something. Thanks."

Hanging up the phone and sharing my live location with Troy, I curved around the property, trying to see in through the windows to get a better idea of what I was dealing with, until I noticed a figure moving up the pathway to the house.

With a jacket on, and a hood over his head and face, the character was unidentifiable. Carefully stepping over twigs and debris that was scattered underneath my feet, I followed around the grounds of the house, hoping to get a better look at the person making their way towards the front door - but it was useless. Slinking up the run-down wooden steps to the entrance, the man kicked the door open, the hinges squeaking under the force - who was he?

I waited, looking over the property, waiting for something.

A GOOD TWENTY minutes had passed, and there was no movement coming from inside or outside of the property. My patience was growing thin, knowing that the person who had killed my best friend was inside played havoc with my mind, all I wanted to do, was go in there and get my hands on him.

The sound of sirens filled the distance, and I didn't give it a second thought. It was London, there were always sirens of police cars and ambulances filling the city. It wasn't unusual, especially in this part of town.

Perching myself on a log, my leg bounced in a mix of frustration and anticipation. I needed to get in there, I had him cornered. If it wasn't for the second bloke turning up, I would have most likely given into temptation and have my fists planted deep into his face by now.

The sound of gravel echoed down the unmade path I'd walked down an hour or so ago, it wasn't footsteps, more like tyres. Standing up and placing myself up against a tree, hiding myself from any other intruders, I kept still, shallowing my breath. Everything out here seemed scarily quiet, and the last thing I wanted to do was go and give myself up, not after I'd been here all this time.

"Take precautions, stay safe." An authoritative voice said. Peering around the rough trunk of the tree, I was met by three police cars and a number of officers with stab proof vests on. They must have figured out the same thing I had. Garrett's killer was in that property, and they were here to get him.

My phone buzzed at the same time the officers made their way down towards the threshold of the house. I opened the message from Troy for the initial information he'd gathered for me.

JAMES SLOANE.

WIFE – CHRISTINA SLOANE (DECEASED)

DAUGHTER - RILEY SLOANE

MEDICAL HISTORY - STAGE FOUR CANCER

I pulled my eyes away from the phone screen as I heard the police make their move. A few seconds later the sound of screams pierced my ears. The terrified screams of a girl.

My body tensed at the sound, my mind automatically thinking back to Lily. I refrained from crashing through the front gate and into the house to find out what was going on, even though it took every ounce of self-control in my being not to do the one thing that felt so natural to me.

Instead, I held my position, and waited—I felt like I'd been waiting around all day—it was exhausting, knowing that I couldn't do what I wanted to. I wanted to kill that fucker, and I wanted to save the girl who was still somewhere inside of the house.

My attention flicked back to the front door as the man from the bar was escorted out by two police officers, he didn't seem to be putting up much of a fight. He followed the orders and made his way to the car, occasionally looking back towards the entrance as though he was waiting for something to happen - for someone to come out behind him.

And they did. Three officers dragged the second man out of the house, now topless, his entire face and body on show.

I knew this person.
Leonard.

Chapter Thirty

"I'm telling you, it's him Dax. There's no doubt about it." Hank paced up and down the tiled kitchen floor, his skin white as anything, like he'd seen a ghost. "He had that scar on his arm. I know for a fact it's him."

Hank's revelation seemed unlikely; firstly, why the hell would Leonard be back in London after all these years, and secondly, how the fuck did we not know about it? I guess, it had been over a decade since everything came out about him and what he did to Lily, and that over time, we just assumed he was far away from this place hiding under a rock, or dead. I think everyone in this room would have preferred the latter option, but according to Hank, that wasn't the case.

"Are you positive it's him?" Kian asked, his temper in a state of undress. He'd never been good at channelling his anger into anything other than, well, anger. His fists were clenched by his sides, and his face a growing shade of red.

Before Hank could answer, Kian bellowed at him again, "I need you to be certain on this. Is it *him*?" he posed the question again.

"Kian, no disrespect, but if I didn't think it was him, I wouldn't have brought it to your attention." He scowled at my brother, as they stared at each other. I don't know why Kian was being so difficult, I trusted Hank with every single part of me. Leonard was out there, Hank knew it, and even though after all this time it seemed extremely peculiar that the bastard was back, Kian needed to get his shit together and keep his cool – if that was even possible.

"Dax, what do you suggest we do?" Shattering the awkward silence that filled the room between the telepathic conversation that my other brother and Hank seemed to be having with their eyes, I asked the question that I hoped would lead to the answer we all wanted to hear.

We get him and we kill him.

"We find him. We reel him in. We get him here. And then we do what we should have done a long fucking time ago." Dax focused the conversation back around, whilst Hank and Kian are still engaged in the stupid staring contest they were having with each other.

Running my hand through my hair and holding onto the back of my neck to reign myself in and stop from jumping to my feet and taking the Glock out of the safe.

My eldest brother was smart, he was most like my dad. He was calm and calculated, even in the most high-powered and stressful situations. He knew that he couldn't just burst into wherever Leonard was being held and plant a bullet deep in his chest. He knew he had to have a plan in place if this was going to work, especially now that he was with the authorities.

"Hank, you said there was a girl at the scene. Any idea on what's happened with her?"

"I'm not sure, but she looked so scared. She was young, twenty at a push, older than Lil-" His words faded off, realising what we were all thinking. Had Leonard gotten his hands on another innocent person? Had he been doing what he did to Lily to someone else?

The idea of this made my stomach swell, I couldn't bear to think of what that poor girl had gone through after knowing what we now know about Lily. My mind filled with thoughts of all the ways my brothers and I would end him. Would the final blow be a gunshot to the face, or a blade across his throat. After years of doing what we do, I knew there were endless ways to inflict maximum pain on someone without them dying, so torture would no doubt be agreed on.

"Do we have a name for the girl?" Dax questioned, clearing his throat.

"I think her name's Riley Sloane. The daughter of James Slone – who, you know…" *Killed our father.* "I got the information from Troy earlier when I found the house."

"Okay good work. We need to find out where she goes to college, who her friends are, where she hangs out. I need to know everything about this girl, text Troy and ask him to get me the information as a matter of urgency."

With that, Hank turned his body towards the door and left with his phone in hand, no doubt to get what my brother had asked for.

"Meanwhile, I'm going to pull a few strings, and find out where Leonard is being held. It'll probably take six months to a year, but we need him out of custody and back on the streets. I've got a plan." Kian and I looked at Dax like he was crazy.

"You want him back out on the streets so he can keep doing what he's been doing?" Kian asked, "Are you fucking stupid?"

The glares between each of them were enough to make

me want to crawl up into a ball and hide away from whatever shakedown was about to happen. They're eyes battling against each other in some secret blood brother duel. I sat there, perched on the side of the desk, just watching, looking over at them both, willing one of them to say something that would let me in on their private disagreement.

Personally, I didn't understand why Dax wanted to eventually let Leonard walk free, he deserved to rot in the hell that was a prison cell. We could have him transferred to the worst prison in the country, one where they prayed on child molesters. We would have made sure that the news got out to the inmates who would ultimately have done the dirty work for us.

God knows that as soon as he was out and in the clear, he'd get his filthy hands on someone else as quick as he could. But I also knew that as a team, we could get vengeance on him, we would be the ones who could personally put an end to him, once and for all, and I guess that was what we all really wanted, even if we had to play the waiting game.

"Okay." Kian finally said. "He can go free, but he'll be under surveillance the entire time." It was almost as though they had communicated with one another outside of these four walls, away from me. They both seemed to understand what it was each other wanted, but I was still at a loss. Unaware of how this master plan of Dax's would work and equally unsure of what role I would be playing in this game. But I was sure about one thing. I was sure about doing whatever I could do to put this animal down.

One Year Later

Chapter Thirty-One

It was coming up to the year anniversary of my father's death, and even though some days were harder than others, most of the time seemed to pass by with no major problems. Somehow each day got easier. It was weird not having him around, and my heart ached knowing that I was never going to be able to see him again.

I had my own idea about grief, and I'd thought that if I just ignored it then it would disappear. But over the course of my life, losing the people that I loved so much, I'd learnt that it didn't just go away. There was no pushing through it or brushing it under the carpet. I had to learn to accept that those people were never coming back, no matter how many times I walked down memory lane just for a few moments with the ghosts of them.

I wished that I had hugged him goodbye before I'd left that day, but there was no point dwelling on the things that I did or didn't do. There was no point hating myself for not saying the things that I should have said. I had to learn to grieve. I had to learn that there was no end to it, it was something that you had to endure. Grief was love, it was love in all forms, love that you could no longer give to the person you wanted to, and I think that was the hardest thing of all.

My brother's and I had managed to sort out his estates, and luckily, because of Dax and Kian's involvement with the parts of my dad's business that I didn't want to lend a hand to, that side of things carried on with very little negative impact on me. The drugs kept flowing in through the docks, and the money kept rolling into both my brother's pockets.

Although I'd been offered some financial handouts from it, I never took a penny. I didn't want to be a part of any of it, and even when I first started out on my business ventures, I made sure that the money my father had offered me wasn't stained with the crimes of drug import and exports. Instead, it came from offshore accounts where he put his payments from other areas of the business, the analytical sides, where people would go to him to find information about predators, or deeper background checks on potential candidates for jobs that my dad's friends were looking to fill.

There was no doubt about it, he was a mastermind in everything that he did, putting everything he had into what he'd already built, alongside any new ventures that might have cropped up. He was an incredible businessman—illegal activities aside—and I know that all three of us longed to be as wise as he was.

By taking over parts of the business, I'd learnt a hell of a lot, from how to run a big scale organisation, making sure staff were paid on the correct times and ensuring we knew how to deal with unhappy clients correctly. Although, unfortunately for Kian, I think any future role in Personal Relations was out of the window. He still, even after all this time, didn't understand that you can't continuously plant your fist into the wall of a client's house and expect to get away with it.

Brandon had also offered his services to us; I had no doubt that he would. Although we kept him out of some of the key details, we didn't tell him that she would be used as leverage, we didn't tell him that she'd experienced the same level of abuse that Lily had. We'd told him that she was the daughter of the man who'd killed our father, and that was enough to get him on board. The file we handed over to him was small, we'd removed some of the main information. At the start it didn't sit right with me that he was in on this job and didn't know the intricacy or know all the details of the plan – but he was hot headed like Kian was, so Dax decided it was for the best that he knew as little as possible.

Over the last year, we had planned out meticulously every stage of this mission. Each of us knew what we had to do down to a tee. It should be plain sailing, as long as we could get our hands on the one person who unknowingly could help us the most.

Riley Sloane.

Little did she know, but she was the key to all of this working out for the best, although I begged to differ that she would think that once she was bundled into the back of one of our vans and taken against her will, but needs must and all that. She'd come round eventually, I had no doubt that once she found out what Leonard had done to Lily, that she would want to help end him nearly as much as we did.

We'd decided not to go after James Sloane; he had terminal cancer, and only had a short amount of time left to live, and as much as I wanted him dead because he'd ruined our lives and took our father from us, the cancer would be punishment enough for what he'd done. At the end of the day, he hadn't gone out to kill my dad, it was a case of wrong place wrong time.

James Sloane wasn't a murderer; he was simply a man who was fucked up in the head because his wife had died and he too was dying. There was no excuse for what he'd done, but our family, more than anyone, should understand the effects that the death of someone you love can have on you.

Riley's story goes that her mother had died when she was only a kid and was left to be brought up by her ex-carpenter father—well that was until he became an alcoholic, no doubt drunk himself into an oblivion after losing his wife—not that I know, but I heard that love could make you do crazy, stupid shit. I'd never been in love; I was too messed up in the head for that. I just fucked who I wanted when I wanted, and that was that. I didn't have time to get caught up in romanticising a life with anyone. I was too focused and probably too highly strung.

She'd grown up living in the same derelict house that Hank had been at a year ago, the day that he'd seen Leonard alive again. Her school records show that her attendance started to drop around the age of fourteen, she was lucky enough to scrape through her exams and be enrolled in the local college. After some time spent looking further into her life, it became apparent that she had very little to no friends. Within the last year she'd managed to get a job in a bar, serving drinks to punters, the bar was a bit better suited to her compared to the ones that her father used to drink in.

She wasn't at the house much either, our people who had been tailing her noticed that she would often go back to the college of hers or spend the nights at random customer's houses. To be honest, I couldn't blame her for not wanting to be at the house. It had taken me a while, and I had only gone through her file once, but after reading about the things that Leonard did to her, I could understand why going home with punters seemed like a better choice than heading back to a house full of nightmares and memories of all the merciless things that had happened to her there.

In a way, everything that she'd been through, all the abuse she'd suffered, should help towards her being easily swayed into helping my brothers and I - and today was the day that our operation went into play.

"BRANDON, ARE YOU READY KID?" Dax said down the phone, relentlessly pacing up and down the main office. The weather was mild for an April day and considering the lead up to today had presented us with a shit load of rain, the sun was shining brightly onto my mother's garden. The roses buds were starting to come out in bloom and the irises had popped up all over the place over the last few weeks.

My mum would have loved this, all this space and all of these flowers, she would have said that it would have put her little windowsill garden to shame.

"Okay, well, you know what you need to do, keep me updated on everything... Yeah, great, speak soon." Dax hung up the phone and placed it on the oak desk by the window.

Everything was ready. Now we just had to wait.

Chapter Thirty-Two

THERE'D BEEN no contact between us and Brandon for nearly two weeks. We had no idea where he was, and he wasn't picking up his phone. We'd been round to check in at his place, but it was empty, everything still in place since I'd checked here three days ago, nothing had been touched.

After his dad had died, he spent most of the time at our house, because we were his family, we were all he had left in this world. He was my best friend, and I would do anything for him, and he knew that.

The fact that there'd been radio silence for all this time made me think the worst had happened, had they both been in an accident, or she'd somehow managed to stab him in the neck with one of those kitchen knives he always had out on display – something I'd told him to hide away, for the exact reason that if someone managed to get in, they were easily accessible to them.

I kicked myself for not changing his father's name to mine on his hospital records as his next of kin. If something had happened to Brandon, they'd be trying to get hold of someone that was now six feet underground. Dead, useless and in a serious state of decay.

Driving around the city, I kept my eyes open for any sight of Brandon or Riley, I'd only seen her photo once, and it was from when she was younger, so it was more than likely that she'd changed a lot since the photo had been snapped. Still, I kept my eyes open, scanning the crowds for Brandon's surfer styled blonde hair, and homing in on anyone that might resemble Riley.

Pulling up outside the bar that Riley had been working at, I caught a glimpse of someone walking out through the large deep red door.

Could that be her?

Dark hair fell down her shoulders and shone in the soon to be fading sun. If this was her, then *fuck* she was beautiful. She turned to wave back to whoever was in the bar, her smile increasing my serotonin—and testosterone levels—causing the inner teenager in me to resurface.

Descending the stairs, she almost bounced her way down, a spring in every step she took, all things considered, she looked happy. She didn't look like the kind of person who had lost her father to a two by three-meter prison cell. Nor did she look like the kind of girl who'd suffered abuse at the hands of the devil incarnate, but then again, who was I to judge what that kind of person looked like. The only insight I'd gotten into what a sexual abuse victim looked like was Lily, and I didn't need reminding that we'd completely missed all the signs. She looked older than nineteen though, so I shook the concept of it being the girl that I so desperately wanted to find.

As I went to pull away from the space, I'd parked the car in outside of the bar, a woman flung the door out and hurried down the stairs.

"Riley, love, you forgot this."
My fuck, it's her.
It's fucking her.

All the notions I had about how stunning the girl was were soon stifled down back inside of me, as I put my business hat back on and threw the car door open. I needed to find out where she was heading, and who she was there with.

Was there any chance that she had escaped Brandon?

If she had, then where the fuck was he?

Making our way through the busy streets, I followed on as she visited some of the market stalls, picking up various items, and occasionally smiling down at her phone.

Who was making her smile like that?

For some stupid fucking reason, a small wave of jealousy crept over me. *Jesus Christ*. This is all going off of the way she looks, and I was definitely thinking with my dick. I needed to remember that her father had mowed my father down with his car and fled the scene. Now was not the time to start getting distracted by the girl with the perfect smile and perky tits. Damn, if my brothers could get a hold of my thoughts as I followed behind her with my eyes focused wholly on her ass, then they'd be beating mine, just like I'd beaten Durham's all those years ago.

As hard as I tried, I couldn't stop myself from looking. She was sensational. As her body weaved in and out between the sea full of people, I found it hard to keep up with her, losing her among the commuters and shoppers.

Focus Tanner. Fucking focus.

Skipping along the cobbled pavement and through one of the city's parks, she was leading me somewhere I wasn't familiar with. I never came to this part of the capital, it wasn't a bad part of London, but it was well out of the way from where any of my businesses were, so I never had the need to travel here.

Turning down onto another busy road as she exited the park, I pulled back, aware that she may have noticed me following behind as we made our way through the floral park. Reaching into her handbag, she pulled out a set of keys and made her way up the stairs of a tall block of apartments, her hair blowing effortlessly in the wind.

"Hey Lucian, how are you?" She asked the security man guarding the main door, her voice, almost angelic, just like the way she carried herself. I knew that there was no way I was getting into the building, not when it looked like something only the rich and famous resided in.

I questioned how she was managing to stay in a place like this. I'd seen the place that she grew up in, it was far from a palace, and there was no way that her salary from the bar would be anywhere near enough to cover the rent on a property like the ones that were homed in this building.

Pulling my phone out of my pocket, I hit the call button, ringing through to Troy's phone, I needed to find out more about this block of apartments, and I needed to know the names of every single person that lived here.

After a brief conversation, I pinged him over the address of the building, and waited on a bench opposite the block. Deep down I knew that it was very unlikely that Riley Sloane's name was going to appear on the list of people who lived here, but maybe there would be something that would help me get to the bottom of where my best friend had disappeared to. At this moment in time, I was more concerned for Brandon's safety, Riley's part in this plan could wait, just until I knew that he was safe.

Chapter Thirty-Three

"You're telling me, he's been keeping her at a place his dad owned? A place that we knew fuck all about?" Kian boomed, his anger about the situation clear to everyone in the room. I nodded in agreement. That's exactly what he's been doing.

I was torn between feeling a sense of relief that Brandon was okay and being pissed that he'd steered away from the plan and failed to do what we'd asked him to do. He didn't know what bigger plan she was part of, and he didn't know that she would be used as bait, the only thing that would help us get to Leonard.

I kicked myself for not keeping him in the loop more, but it was my brothers who had decided it would be better not to tell him, if only for the fact that if he knew why we wanted her, then he might go off course and try to play the hero. He was like that, but ultimately this was something that us three as brothers needed to do, we couldn't have Brandon going off track and finishing a job that we needed to do ourselves.

We would never have known to look for other

properties in his dad's name, he'd been dead for years. I guess that was our mistake for assuming that he only owned the places we'd been to, this one we hadn't ever seen. I questioned why Brandon had never mentioned it to me, and why he'd always lived at his family home, even after he lost his dad.

"Someone needs to go and check the area out more. I need to know the ways in and out, someone call Troy and get him to pull up the blueprints of the building and have him email them over to me." Dax ordered in his *I'm the boss* voice.

"I'll check it out tomorrow, I know what time she finishes work now, and I remember the way there." I offered. It wasn't a lie, I did remember the way there, and how long roughly it took her to make her way from the bar to the apartment block—I had a brain that soaked up information like a sponge—but I also offered up my services just so I could see her again. Fucked up, I know, but something drew me to her.

Probably the fucking sensational views you got walking behind her, jackass.

"Yeah, go tomorrow, see what you can find out, but whatever you do, don't let her see you. If we're going to do this, we need to stick to the plan as much as possible." I nodded agreeing to everything Dax said, even though my brain had other ideas.

Here I was, waiting like a creep outside of the same apartment block as yesterday. I tried hard to blend into the streets, but I still felt like *Joe Goldberg*. Unlike him, I didn't bother to wear a cap to disguise who I was, and in a way, I wanted her to see me, even though in a day or two she'd be bundled into the back of a Lawson van against her will and brought to our house for interrogation.

Checking my watch, aware that she'd be home in a few minutes, I stood up and crossed over the street, dodging the oncoming traffic in the process—you'd think that I would have learnt after my father's death not to play around with moving vehicles—before jumping up the stairs to the building.

Without my brother's knowledge or input, I'd come up with a master plan on how to get into the building and past the security standing on the door. Approaching the entrance, I plastered a friendly smile on my face as the doorman clocked me.

"Hi, I'm new in town, just opening a business a few streets down from here and I was wondering how much these apartments are to rent?" I questioned, my imposter act working as the man started explaining to me who I would need to contact, even kind enough to hand me one of the business cards for the apartment directors, along with his number and email address printed on it.

"If you email him, I'm sure he'd be happy to do business with you." He said offering me a smile. "Oh, and if you could mention my name, that would be great, they might finally decide to offer me a managerial position here if I've helped them gain some more business."

"No problem, Lucian." Internally kicking myself for using the name I'd heard Riley call him yesterday. Luckily for me the shiny gold nametag attached to his suit gave me clearance. "I'll make sure I do, thanks for your help, take care." I waved as I turned to make my way back down the stairs. Without warning, I was face to face with the beautiful enemy, knocking everything out of her hands and onto the floor.

"Damn it. I'm so sorry." I muttered, looking down at the girl that I knew was Riley. Lifting her head and placing her hand over her eyes to protect them from the sunlight, she offered me an apology and quickly bent down to pick up her keys and phone that were now on the concrete steps below us. Luckily her shopping bags had stayed intact, as much as I wanted to speak to her, I didn't have time to be picking up her shopping off of the steps.

Being the true gentleman I was, I bent down to collect her phone and keys and placed them into her hands, our skin grazing against each other, as our eyes met. If this was a movie, you could say that this was one of those 'moments' two main characters have between each other. Pushing the thought to the back of my mind, I offered her a smile, my gaze still pinned to her soul piercing dark eyes that were glistening in the May sunlight.

My work here was done. For now.

Chapter Thirty-Four

I SAT in the chair in my dad's office reeling and playing over the events of last night. After I'd paid a visit to Riley, my brothers joined me in the park across the road from the newly discovered apartment on Brandon's property portfolio. It was agreed, mainly between my two brothers, that Brandon deserved to be punished for keeping Riley from us.

He had been my best friend since we were teenagers, and throughout that time, he'd been as loyal as a fucking dog, so I questioned his motives behind his behaviour, jumping to the conclusion that they were probably the same as what my motive would be. Amazing how tempting pussy can be, right?

So, now, not only had the Sloane family taken a father from us, but they'd also managed to create a divide between me and Brandon which resulted in a serious discussion about his future with us at the hands of my two older brothers. I sat this one out. As much as I was pissed at him, he was still my best friend.

According to Kian, they'd fucked him up. I tried not to

think about it, I had other things on my mind. He'd been given what was coming to him, and now we had to get Riley here. Dax had agreed with Brandon that this morning they would take Riley as she left for work. To be honest, I was at the stage where I just wanted this over with. I wanted her here, I wanted things to get fixed between myself and Brandon, and I wanted Leonard's head on a fucking stake.

I knew it was going to take some time, it wasn't going to be a quick turnaround, nothing was when my brothers and torture were mixed together. We'd once kept someone alive for over two weeks, inflicting pain on them every day until their body gave out. It was experimental as Kian, my sick and twisted fucked up brother, put it.

The sun was only just starting to rise, it was early, but I knew that we still had to drive into the city and wait for Riley to leave the apartment. Brandon was going to make sure to distract the doorman so we could get her into the van as quick as possible without being detected. I don't know if they'd promised him something for helping out, but I knew this would be the last time he and my brothers would ever work together. They had a way of using people to their advantage and then dropping them when they proved no more use to them.

Standing up and making my way to the kitchen, my body craved coffee, and luckily enough for me, Grace had already been up and put some in the press ready for when I wanted a cup. This was a usual thing she did on days where she knew we had early jobs and my body thanked her for it each time.

Trailing over to the French patio doors at the end of the kitchen, the windows amplified the warmth of the sunlight that glared over the horizon, highlighting the colours of the flowers in the gardens outside. Unlocking the door and carefully pushing it open I stepped outside, breathing in the fresh air. The quiet of the morning opposed the crimes we had and would commit, but being here in this moment, made my head feel lighter, a melodic calm washing over me as I thought about all the things that would go down over the next few weeks.

I wished my dad was here. If he was, then I wouldn't be getting ready to kidnap the unbelievably pretty brunette I'd crashed into yesterday.

Chapter Thirty-Five

HER SCREAMS FILLED the back of the van. She was pissed, and I was strangely turned on by the burst of attitude she was displaying. My brother had chucked a bag over her head, classic kidnap behaviour. She wouldn't shut up, no matter how hard I internally yelled at her to. There was only one way that this was going to end - her being knocked the fuck out.

I couldn't quite look at Brandon as my brothers stood speaking to him, I would have kept my mouth shut if it wasn't for my brother's coaxing me into saying something.

"We don't owe you shit." I responded as he begged us to let him keep his job. Unbeknown to him, he would always be my best mate, but I also had two unruly brothers that I needed to keep up appearances for. Once all this shit was over, we could sort out our differences and get back to normal. He'd done so much for me over the years that it would be hard for me to just up and leave without giving a shit. Unlike my brothers, I knew what it felt like to have no one, and I didn't want that for Brandon - I would make sure that wasn't the case when it came to me and him. He would always have me, just like he always had done.

With Riley still screaming in the back, Kian's temper was rising. His face turning cherry red, and his fists tightening, turning his knuckles white. He'd demanded that she shut up a fair few times, but this girl was relentless, so Kian did what he knew best. Opening the door to the van, Riley on show with her potato sack covered head, my brother took his gun from his holster and smashed her round the head with it, sending her to the floor of the van before slamming the doors shut again.

He was ruthless at the best of times, but hitting a girl was something I'd never seen him do, nor did I want to see again. My dad had always taught me never to hit a girl, and I knew for a fact he'd be turning in his grave full of disappointment if he could have seen what the anger had just led to Kian doing. As much as it went against every moral I had, I knew that I couldn't jump in and stop Kian from what he was doing. I knew he was still hurting over my dad, but I also knew that it wasn't Riley's fault - none of this was.

Now that we had her, we could kick start the plan back into action. Driving through the early morning to one of our warehouses on the other side of the city, my mind wandered to how scared Riley must be. Nothing about this situation sat right with me, but I knew that it was required so we could avenge Lily, and make Leonard pay for the heinous acts he'd put her through. Knowing he'd done the same to Riley would help our plan fall into place. We needed her, more than she needed us, not that we'd spin it like that to her.

Her case worker had been told by one of our insiders that Leonard had been killed in prison, which is probably the reason that she looked so relaxed walking the streets of London. Telling her that he was dead meant that she'd unwind more, leaving us to work on the rest.

Our plan was messed up, we were using a victim as leverage to get what we wanted. That in itself bordered on some kind of abuse, and deep down, I understood that when she found out that Leonard was still alive, mentally she would crumble, how could she not? Unlike my brothers, especially hot-headed Kian, I had some kind of conscience, not that I was acting that way.

As we pulled into the grounds of the warehouse, I reminded myself that that's all I was doing - *acting*. This wasn't the person I truly was. Okay, so I'd killed a few people, but what's the big deal, they were monsters that prayed on the vulnerable. My brothers and I liked to play God, and we were doing the world a favour by eradicating them, I saw that as something that contributed to the greater good.

Even with my morals somewhat skimming the remanence of my soul, I dragged Riley out of the back of the van, she was still laying there, lights out with that god awful potato sack over her pretty little head. I rolled my eyes as I threw her over my shoulder and carried her into the warehouse, propping her up on the metal chair that sat in the middle of the large damp room. It was eery enough being in here as one of the joint owners of the building, so I couldn't imagine how she was going to feel when she finally came round and realised that she was now in an unfamiliar place, unable to see her surroundings.

I felt sad for her, sad that she'd gone through everything that Lily had and sad that she was now sat here being left in the hands of my brothers because of something she had zero control over. Things like this just proved how unfair life was, and how, that at any moment, the life you once knew could change in a split second. I knew this more than anyone. I'd had the rug pulled from underneath me one too many times, but, whatever I did to try and stop myself from falling, never worked. Instead, it found me in a dingy warehouse, with a nineteen-year-old girl strapped to a chair in front of me, probably terrified for her life.

We weren't going to kill her, that was never and will never be part of the plan, but she didn't know that, and sometimes the uncertainty of a situation can be scarier than the actual outcome. Still, here I was, regretful, and somewhat wishing I could take Riley away from this place. I should hate the girl sitting here. Her dad had killed mine, but somehow, she made everything feel fresh, she didn't know my past, she didn't know the trauma I'd endured, and she probably had no idea that I knew all about hers.

But I knew *everything*.

Chapter Thirty-Six

"Ouch! That hurt you shithead!" I couldn't help but contain the laughter that sat in my throat, caused by Riley's attitude towards my brothers. It was weird seeing someone argue with them and freely give them a piece of their mind. Everyone was always so polite and addressed both of them with such respect it would put the Queen to shame. It was sickening really.

Yet, seeing two hard-faced men being spoken to like shit by a five-foot something fiery brunette, was comical. She clearly had no idea of the power they held over people or the kinds of things they were most definitely not afraid of doing. I wondered whether she'd act the same way if she knew that last week Kian had carved the word 'cunt' into the back of someone with a rusty flick knife before slicing open their stomach. I doubted that she'd hold up the same persona as the one she was throwing around right now.

I watched on as she spouted a string of abuse in their direction, careful not to chuckle out loud. I had to give it to the girl - she had bigger balls than most men in the city, and she wasn't afraid of making my brothers aware that she was pissed at them.

After she'd had her crazy little outburst, her eyes flicked between the three of us, no doubt studying our faces and making a mental note of identifiable features for if she managed to escape from us. Pinning her eyes on me, her face dropped.

"I know you."

Okay Tanner, time for action.

"Well, you're a clever girl aren't you, *Dulce Venganza*?" Throwing in a bit of Italian for effect, I cringed at myself. *Sweet Vengeance.* I hated this fucking version of myself some days. After speeling off a number of lies about how we'd been following her for the last couple of weeks I broke away from the triangular formation my brothers and I were stood in, puffing my chest out in an attempt to seem somewhat intimidating.

When asked if she knew who the Lawson brothers were, her response was unexpected and dripped with complete sarcasm with a side of *I don't give a fuck* sass. Internally commending her on her bravery, I couldn't stop my eyes from falling down to where she was sitting, staring right into hers. Eyes that were filled with something that I'd never seen in a person before, she really didn't care if she lived or died, and if I had to put money on it, I'd put it all down on the colour that said she believed the only way she would make it out of here was in a body bag.

After my brothers toyed with her a little more, they decided to fill her in on one bit of information she didn't know about. They disclosed it was our father that her dad had killed. She looked so innocent, so afraid, so taken aback by this newly discovered detail that I thought she might throw up.

"I'm sorry." She sniffled, and once again, my heart bled for the girl in front of me. I knew it shouldn't, but it did. Like myself, she'd suffered loss just like I had, her mother first, then her innocence and now her own damn father. We probably had more in common with each other than we would ever admit to, but this wasn't a first date, I wasn't here to make a connection with her, and she wasn't here to ask me questions about what my upbringing was like in life. She wouldn't look at me in the same light if she knew, she'd probably feel sorry for me, empathetic at the fact that we'd lost both of our parents way before their time.

Before anyone could say anything, Kian strode forward towards Riley, hands gripped in tight fists, and planted one into the side of her face directly onto her cheekbone. Blood flew from her mouth, as her head followed through the direction of Kian's attack.

I do not want to watch this.

Momentarily, I blacked out, defocusing my eyes and looking beyond what was happening in front of me. Wishing away everything that was happening in this cold warehouse. Wishing so hard that I could find a time machine and use it to jump forward to a stage when all of this was over. To a time when we'd already finished Leonard. To a place where Riley was sitting in a house somewhere in front of an open fire reading a book. I lost count of how many times Kian used the brute of his fists to rain down onto Riley's body.

Snapping myself out of the idealistic made-up world I'd found myself creating in my head and back to the shit show reality that was playing out in front of me like a cheap horror film, I interrupted Kian's vicious punches.

"She's done." I sounded pathetic, there was zero substance or command in those words, all I knew was that I needed to say something, anything to stop him. He didn't. Instead, he reared his fist back in a bid to serve her one final blow directly into her stomach. I wanted to jump in and smash my brother in the face with my fists, which I realised had formed unknowingly to me among the brutality.

"Kian. Enough."

Thank you, Dax.

If there was anyone left in the world that Kian might listen to, it was our eldest brother. Dax knew how unruly Kian could be, and over the years he'd picked up on how to somewhat control him, learning from our father.

"We don't want her dead." He carried on, and I let out a deep exhale in relief. "Not yet anyway," he snarled.

Wait. What?

Chapter Thirty-Seven

I TRIED to keep myself busy over the next day, but I couldn't concentrate on anything. I had taxes to sort out and wages to pay to my employees, yet it seemed my mind would constantly revert back to Riley, wondering if she would actually make it out of this plan alive. We'd agreed that she would, but after our encounter with her, I wasn't too sure if this still stood.

I dare not ask Dax if he meant what he said about her not being dead - yet. I couldn't let on that I was concerned that this master plan would suddenly take a turn and come crashing down like a hijacked plane. We never got attached to people, that's not how we did business, and it was probably for the best.

We were due to visit her again today, but Kian was nowhere to be seen, he'd taken one of the vans and turned the tracker off. My stomach filled with dread as Dax tried his phone for what felt like the millionth time this morning.

"He's with *her*. There's nowhere else that he'd be." I explained to Dax, knowing deep down that's where I'd wanted to be for the last twenty-four hours, making sure that she was okay, and maybe even tending to the wounds on her perfectly crafted face. I don't know why he assumed that Kian would be anywhere else, he was out for blood, vengeance for our father, and she was the closest thing to James Sloane.

"I swear on my life, I'm going to kill him myself if he doesn't get his shit together." Dax muttered, standing up, straightening out his suit jacket and strolling towards the door. Before he could reach for the door handle, the door flew open, and in entered Kian. Panting and covered in blood. Dax gripped his fist around Kian's shirt and backed him up against the wall next to the door, knocking over one of the many tiffany lamps that lived in the house, the fall resulting in the stained-glass shattering across the floor.

"You better not have touched her. If you've harmed her, or worse, killed her, I will never forgive you." Dax growled, almost frothing at the mouth. Kian battled to get him off of him, but Dax was so filled with anger, that the adrenaline I assumed to be flowing through his body, resulted in a superhuman strength. I'd never witnessed my brothers at each other's throats like this, although they'd get mad at each other, I'd never seen this much anger between them both, and in all honesty, it made me feel slightly awkward.

"It's Brandon. She shot him." He spat back, pressing his head against my eldest brother's. "He's fucking dead!" He strangled out, trying to gather enough oxygen to refill his lungs.

With my feet glued to the floor, I couldn't do anything except stand there, my eyes widening at Kian's announcement. My best friend was *dead*. My mouth suddenly went dry, even if I wanted to say something, I wouldn't have been able to. I felt like I'd eaten a fuck tonne of sand. Trying to peel my tongue off of the roof of my mouth and move the concrete blocks that my legs had morphed into, my brothers carried on speaking, the words not registering in my head.

Coming round from the state of shock, I managed to catch the end of the conversation.

"He was trying to break her out. She went to shoot me, and he jumped in the way." He explained, now finally released from my brother's monstrous hold.

"Where's the body, Kian?"

"It's still there, I sent one of the contractors to clear it up."

Usually, a job like that would be down to Hank and Brandon, but for obvious reasons, they'd grown close over the years, Hank treated us all as though we were his own, and especially over the last year since dad died, so the option of having Hank go and clean up this mess was off the table.

"I need to get out of here." I mumbled, staggering out of the door and towards the gardens. I couldn't breathe, the air was stifling, and my body shook from head to toe. Loosening my tie and collapsing onto the sandstone patio, I gasped for air, desperate to get myself under control.

Why couldn't he just leave her alone, was he really so besotted by the girl that he'd actually given his life for her. As poetic as it was, it was also the most idiotic thing that he'd ever done, and there'd been a fair few dumbass things that he'd done over the course of our friendship. But nothing that had cost him his life.

"Get her back here now." Dax ordered my brother.

"She's already downstairs."

Here we fucking go.

Chapter Thirty-Eight

Two Weeks Later

I still couldn't believe he was dead. I couldn't believe that the girl who was now being held captive in another one of our secret underground rooms was the one who had killed him - instead of killing my brother.

A small service had been held for him at our house, with the remaining staff we had on our books who knew him. I sat the whole time barely saying a word to anyone, to onlookers who had no idea of the situation I probably looked like the rudest person on the planet, only nodding when someone addressed me.

Truth is, even after everything, each bout of loss and grief, each time it hit me harder than the last, you'd think I'd be used to it and have a hard skin when it came to the people I loved dying one by one. I sat on the garden bench my dad had made in memory of my mum, taking in the songs of the birds and the sun that was slowly rising on the horizon. I wondered what my life might have been like if I'd been born to someone who had treated me as important in their life as my mum had treated drugs. I wondered what it would have been like if I'd managed to get a normal job, and met a normal girl, and had a normal wedding and bought a normal fucking house. Probably boring as fuck, but at least I wouldn't have to deal with this shit day in and day out.

Everything that I'd been through and all of the tragedy that had mapped my life out had made me the man I was. It had taught me valuable lessons and to never take things for granted. You never knew what was going to happen, you never knew when it might be the last time you'd speak to someone, or hug them, or just simply exist by their side.

I found it hard to accept that the organ in my chest was still beating when I'd had it broken over and over again. I thought it would have given up a long fucking time ago, but yet, here I was, still breathing, still hurting, and still angry at the world I lived in.

Everyone around me kept dying, and I started to think that it was to do with me more than them. I felt like I had the Grim Reaper on my back, lurking in the darkness until I formed attachments with someone, then *bam*, out came the hatchet which rained down, taking them from me with complete bloodshed.

I couldn't blame it on everything I'd been a part of since walking into that room when I was a young man, and I couldn't put it down to ridding the world of the monsters that, as a family, we were fortunate enough to do something about. It started way before that shit, I was only a kid when the man above decided that my mum had served her time on this planet.

I must have been a real bastard in another life, that was the only thing that could explain why these things kept happening. No one in my life deserved the things that had happened to them. The fear of forming a relationship with anyone else like I'd had with those who were no longer with us, made me feel uneasy, and the emotion that brewed up inside of me when I thought about it wasn't worth the anxiety and stress, so I always parked the idea of being with someone and loving someone in the back of my head.

Sorrow sat heavy on my heart, the weight shrouding me, pulling me down to a place that I didn't want to be in—a place that had the ability to end me if I let it—and some days, that option seemed fairly attractive. At least there I wouldn't be exposed to the desolation and melancholy that filled my still beating heart.

I wondered if my brothers felt the way that I did, I wondered if Riley felt like it. Or did they have a thicker skin than me? Were they able to cope better than I could? I'd never seen my brothers cry over Lily, even when our father died, they didn't show how upset they were for too long, and the day that I first lay eyes on Riley's face, she didn't look anything but happy.

She didn't look how I felt.

She looked how I longed to feel.

Happy.

Letting my eyes wander off into the horizon, I let myself miss them. I let myself feel the pain that I'd been holding in for so long. I needed this, I need to let myself unravel and process all of the war inside me. If I didn't then I knew that there was no other way out of this.

I remembered my mum; and everything that she'd been through. Her life was difficult. Her life caused her pain, which in turn, she placed onto my little shoulders.

I remembered Lily; and thought about everything that she'd gone through at the hands of a person my dad trusted the most. I thought about how scared she must have been, how whatever was going on made her believe that she couldn't speak to us. She was worried about our reactions, scared at what might have happened if she'd spoken about that piece of shit who had put his evil hands on her.

I thought about my father; how he'd saved me when I was a kid and brought me into the family, treated me like I was his own and watched me grow up into the person that he'd had a great deal of input into creating. He had done everything for me, everything and more, more than any father would have done for their sons. He'd shown me what it was like to be loved by someone, and what it was to give love back.

When I'd lost my mum, I was scared to let myself form attachments with anyone else, in fear that they would leave or be taken from me. But looking back at it now, what kind of life would I have had if I hadn't let myself love people? As much as it hurt to lose them, I was happy that I was given the chance to love and be loved, happy that I was able to feel the warmth of a hug from those people. Imagine living a life without that.

I reminded myself that it's a special thing to be able to feel things so strongly. I told myself that if I had closed myself off from love, on any level, then I wouldn't have made it very far without it, I would have been a very sad and lonely person, never having experienced it.

It's true, it does make the world go round, and without it, it would be a very desolate and dark place, a place that would be filled with terror and dejection. So why would you not let yourself love, even if it's only for a short amount of time.

I missed them all, so terribly, but at least I had them once upon a time.

Chapter Thirty-Nine

TODAY OPERATION *WHATEVER-IT-WAS* BEGUN AGAIN after the slight blip we encountered at the start of it. My brothers wanted her there for dinner tonight. Whether she'd agree to it was a different question, and quite frankly, I wasn't holding out much hope. It was clear that she hated us, Kian especially.

She'd tried to shoot him for fuck's sake.

I knew that we needed to do this though. I knew that we needed to use her to get him back, without her, we wouldn't be able to lure him out from wherever the fuck he was now hiding. My brother had initiated the plan for Leonard's release, which made me feel uneasy in itself, but since being released from prison he'd managed to escape the eyes we had on him. He was a ghost again, meaning that it was possible for him to get his hands on someone else. It was even more important that we followed the strategy as meticulously as we'd planned it.

It made my skin crawl. He needed to be put down, like a dangerous fucking animal, and I couldn't wait to have the pleasure of doing it alongside my brothers. In memory of

Lily, and all the other innocent lives he'd corrupted, Riley being one of them.

We needed to get her into the dining room at least, and have a civil conversation with her, explaining everything. Why we'd bought her here, why we needed her help and what she needed to do. My brothers had also agreed that once she'd helped us do what we needed to do then she would be free to leave this place, offering her a place to live, and basically setting her up for life.

If she wanted it, there would be a job for her at one of my businesses. Not that I thought she would take it. Why would she want to still be tied to one of the Lawson trio after what we'd done to her? I guess I wouldn't know until it was offered up, and I suppose if it was Kian that gave her the option it would be shut down straight away, maybe I could give her a bit of hope whilst all this played out. There was no way in hell that she'd want to work for him, not after he'd beaten the living shit out of her, and definitely not after she'd tried to shoot him, killing Brandon instead.

Those were the finer details though.

I knew my brother's had a wildcard up their sleeve, and they'd just threaten her more if she didn't agree to help us, so I needed to do what I could to make sure it didn't come to that. I don't think them threatening to kill her father or throw her back onto the streets for Leonard to get to her would help the situation, we had to tread carefully, which unfortunately didn't come easy to any of us.

Kian was a missile, and he had a knack for ruining things and making situations harder for people than deemed necessary. He didn't have a switch in his head that told him to stop and pull back on the anger that built up inside of him. Once he got to that stage, he was hard to control. He didn't care about other people, all he knew was that most of the time, his threats and violence would get him what he wanted - I hate to admit that it normally worked.

This was a sensitive case though, and Riley had clearly been through more than any girl her age should have been. I wished that Kian would see her as though she was Lily. They'd been in the same position, I just prayed that when she was sat with us tonight, he'd pull his head out of his ass and notice that she had also been a victim, and that our father wasn't killed because of her, she was just the unfortunate offspring of the messed-up alcoholic that had.

"I'll go down and get her." I offered, pulling on my fingers nervously like I was a toddler about to get in trouble. I wanted to speak to her before either of my brothers got the chance to. I had to make sure that she knew it would be better if she just did as they asked, making it easier for everyone involved, especially her.

"That's fine. Bring her into us when you come up. I want to have a chat with her before you show her to her room. Grace is getting it ready for her now." Dax said, sipping on a crystal glass full of whiskey.

I'd never been one for drinking, but I knew that the brown stuff in the glass was good, so I didn't mind having one now and then. In moderation it was fine, but I always worried that I might have an addictive personality like my mum, and there was no way I would be putting myself in an early grave because I couldn't control my urges like her.

"Sure, that's fine." I replied, hoping that my voice didn't crack. It wasn't fine. There was no mention of them having a friendly *chat* with her until this evening. Now, my plan to speak to her privately had gone out of the window. Still, I needed to say something to her in a bid to reassure her. Spinning on my heels, I strode towards the door, closing my eyes in an attempt to control my frustration, and left the room before I exploded.

Being kept under the house on the side nearest the office, my brothers thought it was best that she stayed as close to the place they spent most of their time in case she somehow managed to escape the dungeon they'd thrown her in. She was like a princess in a book, being kept captive by the evil protagonist, and I wondered whether she hoped a knight in shining armour might come and rescue her, or if she'd given up on the idea. I mean Brandon tried but ended up dying in the process.

Did she have anyone else that might try to save her?

I doubted it.

WALKING ALONG THE LAVISH CORRIDORS, that still gave me the creeps even after all these years, you'd think I'd be used to it, I'd lived here most of my life, but the hallways were filled with an air of terror. Maybe it's because I felt the presence of all the people who'd been killed under the floorboards of the property.

Each of us carried a chain which housed the keys to each of the locked rooms, some larger than others, and each colour coded so we didn't waste time figuring out which key unlocked which door. It was something that I'd had to learn pretty quickly when I was given the *privilege* of being handed them.

Flicking through the metal, I pulled the blue coded key away from the rest of the bunch, rubbing my fingers between the grooves, as I finished my journey to the chamber Riley was in. It made me feel like shit knowing that she had been down there for the last twelve days being held captive like a caged animal. She'd been fed, and to be honest, the food we served her was probably better than anything she'd eaten since her dad started to neglect her. She'd been kept in the dark, with no one to speak to, her food being passed through the door, and she was sleeping on a mattress that had been used to keep people we'd tortured on. I knew full well that it was probably covered in various bodily fluids.

Shaking my head, I needed to pull myself together before heading down there. I didn't know what to expect, I didn't know how I would find her. Had she been eating what we'd given her, or had she starved herself in protest?

Pushing away the mirror that covered the secret doorway, I forced the key into the lock and turned it, a loud clicking sound drilling through my ears reminding me of all the times I'd been down here. Opening the door and stepping into the darkness, I used the light of my phone to guide my way down the stairs, and thanked my brothers for putting her in a room where the stairs weren't like the wooden ones that led down to the place we would commit our vigilante obligations in.

The sound of my shoes tapped against the concrete steps of the musky smelling corridor that led down to another door. This one the heaviest out of any of the others due to the fact the room was used to hold people who might try and escape.

Taking a deep breath in, I settled myself down before turning the lock with the same key I'd used on the door above me. We'd had each of the linking rooms fitted with the same lock as the one that led down to it, again, making it easier and quicker for us to enter and exit when we needed to.

Pushing hard on the door to the chamber, I shoved my phone back into my pocket and put my foot over the threshold, stepping into the room. I knew that any form of light would hurt her eyes, and I didn't want to blind the poor girl, I think being kept down here for this period of time was torturous enough.

I could hear her sobs and my own heart jackhammering in my chest as I stilled my body in the dark - she was still alive at least, but that's all I knew. I had no idea what state she was in.

"Riley." I whispered, pulling myself in at the core and straightening my back. No idea why I thought I needed to put on the physical persona of the person people were so used to seeing me as, appearances didn't matter right now, not when I was standing in a cell of ink blank filling the space.

Her breath hitched, and my heart sunk at the sound of her.

Alive. Breathing.

Sad. Tortured.

The sound of my dad's voice darted around in my head.

Every action has a consequence, Tanner, this is something you need to remember.

I got that - but this, right here, this wasn't a consequence that Riley should have had to endure at the stupidity of her father.

Taking my phone out of my pocket, I angled the light down onto the floor slightly. I couldn't see shit in this place.

I needed to get to her, and fuck knows what I risked treading on if I went in blind.

"I'm sorry." Her words bit into my ears, the sorrow in

her voice was almost too much to deal with. I didn't want her apologies, not for the same reason my brothers didn't, but because she was apologising for something she had no control over. She didn't kill my dad. She didn't rape Lily. She was just a bystander in all of this, and whilst I was having my own hand of pain and suffering dealt to me like an evil game of roulette, she too was getting hers. All chips on red. Losing everything when black rolled in.

"Let's get you out of here." I said softly, placing my hand on her waist and leading her out of the darkness.

And I hoped that she would understand why she was here when we arrived with my brothers.

Chapter Forty

My eyes stayed trained on her as she sat in the chair at the opposite end of the table to where my brother was seated. Her eyes darted around the room while she was sipping on the good stuff Dax had offered her. Somehow, I knew that it would take more than a glass of expensive whiskey to sway her, especially when she got bratty with me when I explained we wanted her to work for us. She laughed in the face of danger.

Our faces.

"I don't want to kill anyone," she hurried to say, her tongue gliding over her lips as her eyes flicked to mine as if she wanted some reassurance, treating me like her safe space. Maybe she knew I wasn't the same as my brothers.

She wouldn't have to kill anyone; my brothers wouldn't let her; they wouldn't want to risk her messing it up. This was something they would want to do themselves, making sure the job was done correctly, and so they could make sure it was them who ended his life. She would understand that when she flicked through the file that had just been placed on the table in front of her.

I kept my eyes on her as she took another sip from the crystal glass and proceeded to open the cream file, her face dropping in shock as she turned to the first page. The page that had Leonard's face printed on. The face of a monster. The face of her abuser.

I could almost hear her heart shattering in her chest as she stared down at the page in front of her, exposing the realisation that, even after thinking he was killed in prison, she now knew he was still alive. He wasn't dead. We knew that for a fact, and now, so did she.

My brothers continued with their conversation, explaining what had happened, how Leonard had wormed his way into my baby cousin's life and then taken it from her. How he abused her to the point of death. The expression plastered over Riley's face slowly picked away at my heart, she didn't give anything else away except the fact that she was shocked at this revelation – rightly so. I don't know how long she'd sat there staring down at his picture, time seemed to alter when she was in my presence. Eventually she drew her eyes away from the file, finding mine without hesitation in the room that we were sat in.

Help me, they begged.

Swallowing down the lump in my throat, I asked Hank to escort her to her room located on the next floor. At least if she was to get anything from today, it would be a good night's sleep - if she managed to drift off at all. My mind was whirring, and I couldn't even begin to comprehend what was going through hers. All I knew was that she seemed as though she wanted to get out of here.

With her face now a shade of ghostly white, the blush in her cheeks that I'd noticed on the first day I bumped into her had faded. The joy that once filled those obsidian black eyes was gone, there was nothing left in them except shades of sorrow and despondency. Standing on her feet, I could see her body shaking. Hank placed his hand on her shoulder, offering his support, but she shook it off, slightly jumping under his hand.

After suffering years of abuse at the hands of Leonard, it must be hard for her to be touched by another man, and now she found herself stuck in a house full of them, minus the exception of Grace, who she had yet to meet. If she had the same effect on Riley as she did me, I knew that she would help make her feel at ease as much as she could. She had that about her, the ability to calm someone even in the most stressful of times. It was one of the reasons that I would do anything for her.

Sighing as Riley left the room, I loosened the tie around my neck, flicking open the top button with my clammy hands. Although I knew this was only the beginning, and that we had a lot of work to do until we reach our end goal, I was fucking glad this part was over. My brothers wanted her to join us for dinner later, so that would be the second task I'd have to get her to agree to, understanding it wouldn't be easy for either her or me.

I had a few things I needed to see to today, so I'd think of how to approach this in the best way whilst I was out and about dealing with business. I decided as soon as I'd seen her stumble out of the hole in the wall earlier, that the girl who came across fiery and full of herself was truly vulnerable, and coming down hard on her, like Kian had done, would get us nowhere - well, not anywhere any of us wanted to be.

I had to make her feel safe whilst maintaining some stupid form of dominance over her, I had to show her that we weren't the bad guys, even though she was understandably one hundred percent certain that we were. I had to get her to trust me, and after this long string of male induced trauma over the years, I guessed that would be the trickiest part.

Chapter Forty-One

"I won't let them hurt you, *Dulce Venganza*." I repeated as I asked her again if she'd thought about what my brothers had requested of her. I added to my bout of backhanded begging, asking her if she knew what would happen if she disagreed to help. I believed she thought that we would kill her, but the truth of the matter was that the option she would be exposed to would be *him*. Leonard would be able to get to her if she chose not to work alongside of us.
Without our protection, she would be left alone, and we wouldn't be able to look out for her - well, we could, but my brothers would choose not to.

Leonard wasn't stupid, he'd gone under the radar for over a decade already, and even with our people working day in and day out, we still failed to track the mother fucker down. He was out and incognito once again, probably staying there for a while plotting his next move. Ultimately, Riley had had him thrown into prison, that's how he would see it anyway, completely ignoring the fact that it was because he'd forced himself on a minor. He would want revenge, and no doubt he would get it.

If she didn't agree to help us, and got out of this alive, the concept of looking over her shoulder twenty-four hours a day would in the end drive her insane. She would spend the rest of her time alive worrying about the day that Leonard caught up with her.

She wasn't a silly girl, and he wasn't a silly man. The only upside Leonard would have on Riley if she didn't want to help us, was that he wouldn't have to battle with us to get to her. She needed to understand that we would help protect her at all costs—myself more than Dax and Kian— but I would make sure that she was safe, from Leonard *and* my brothers.

"I will help you," she mumbled staring out of the window. My eyes darted towards her, focusing on her mouth where her teeth grazed along her bottom lip. Her perfectly arched lips.

"I need to do this, not for you or your brothers, but for Lily." I'm not quite sure if she'd grasped the fact that I knew about her past, if she did then she was brave for letting me in the way she was.

We sat for some time, looking over my mum's garden, and I couldn't keep myself from occasionally peering over at her. Taking in the way her hair fell down over her shoulder in waves, lapping against her cheeks when she moved. Admiring the way the orange tint from the setting sun cast shadows on parts of her face, radiating something inside of her that I wanted more of.

This was the first time I'd seen her for who she was, completely exposed. She didn't seem guarded or angry, she didn't have the tightness wrapped around her small frame like she had done on the previous occasions I'd been in her presence. Instead, she was relaxed, and seemed deep in thought about something of amusement, from time to time letting the corners of her mouth tip upwards into a smile, then dipping her head, allowing the waves of brown hair to partially cover her face from me, momentarily building the guarded walls back up around her. I could have sat there forever staring at her beauty, but I needed to shake this weird attachment that I was forming with the enemy's daughter. It wouldn't end well for either of us. Standing up abruptly, I brushed my hands over my suit, remembering that I still had my tie loosely hanging around my neck.

So much for keeping up appearances.

"Dax and Kian will be expecting you downstairs for dinner in an hour." Noticing that she'd been in the same clothes since the day we bundled her into the back of the van—however long ago that was—I offered her a shower and Grace had already helped Hank to choose some outfits for Riley, she'd need something other than her baggy t-shirts whilst living here - even though she did look kind of cute in them.

Chapter Forty-Two

"Is that an order, Tanner?"

God this girl had sass.

Perching on the edge of the queen-sized bed in her newly acquired room, she snapped her eyes to mine as I waited for her to stand up and show me the sleek black dress I'd had Grace hang up for her to wear this evening.

"It's *Sir,* to you." I relayed back, trying to stifle down whatever the fuck feeling it was that seemed to be stirring something in my trousers. Raising a brow and holding her gaze, between narrowed eyes, for as long as she held mine, I waited for another smart-mouth reply.

"Is that an order, *Sir?*"

Jesus fucking Christ. This girl was going to be the death of me.

Within the space of having a shower and putting on the damned dress, she'd flipped her whole *poor me* attitude on its head, and now took on the confident bad-ass sass queen act instead. I didn't know what I preferred most - both of them made me lose a little bit of myself the more time I spent around her.

"Why don't you just shut that pretty mouth of yours and do as you were told like a good girl?" Her face dropped at my response, and she did nothing but stare at me, a hint of surprise in those deep eyes that appeared to have a little bit of their sparkle returning.

If it made her feel better acting like a brat, then that was fine by me. After seeing her in her most vulnerable state, I welcomed this version with my arms opened wide. I wasn't a pig; I knew how to treat women.

Noticing that she'd made some attempt to cover up the remainder of the bruise around her eye made the pit of my stomach twitch, part of me angry at Kian for ever putting his hands on her, but he was my brother, and she was the enemy's daughter. My loyalties lie with him more than they would ever lie with her, but that didn't mean I had to agree with what he'd done.

Grabbing for my extended hand, the touch of her skin seared against mine, our hands fitting perfectly together. Still holding onto her, I took a step back and admired the vision in front of me.

Now that's what a gangster's wife is meant to look like.

Fuck.

Big fucking mistake, Tanner.

I cursed my brain for even putting that stupid thought there in the first place, but I couldn't deny that she pulled the dress off exquisitely. My eyes wandered from her face and down to her feet, stopping at the most important parts for a second longer than I probably should have, her nipples showing slightly through the silk of the midnight black dress.

My Adams apple bobbed ferociously in my throat as I looked down at her, my stature still towering over her even though she had heels on... Until she didn't. Clearly not a fan of heels, the girl who—thirty seconds ago—had been giving me a pop of her new personality had now clumsily fallen into me, the smell of her clean skin invading my senses, the softness of her freshly washed hair brushing against my face.

I don't know why I felt the need to hold onto her longer than required, but as she writhed and wriggled in my arms, I held onto her tighter, before finally releasing her and placing her back on the bed to take a look at her ankle.

After a quick analysis and concluding she'd sprained it, I pulled her up off of the bed to face me.

"You look stunning by the way." The words slipped off my tongue before I could even process what I was saying.

Idiot.

Riley tipped her head up to meet my gaze, our faces now inches from each other, our eyes studying each other closely, and I couldn't help but want to kiss her. I shouldn't want to kiss her, but fuck, she looked insatiable standing there, wide-eyed and slightly out of breath.

Double idiot.

Thankfully—I *think*—Grace interrupted another one of those romance novel *moments*. Acknowledging her, I thanked her for letting us know that dinner was about to be served in the large dining room, another place in this house Riley had yet to visit.

"I know you think I'm dangerous *Dulce Venganza* but trust me." I couldn't help but open my mouth, yet again, stupidly trying to play some kind of mobster Romeo in this pathetic story of ours.

Ding ding ding, you've just won the prize for idiot of the year.

Pulling herself away from my grip, she turned on her heels, leaving me to stand there absent from her presence.

Shoeless, she made her way to the doorway, following after Grace out into the hallway for dinner, questioning how much of the food we'd left her had actually been eaten.

She paused briefly, peering back at me over her shoulder, and for a moment I wished that she'd come running back into my arms, playing out a scene you'd *definitely* find in a book sat on the shelf of the romance section in a library.

"And for the record, I'm not your *Dulce Venganza*."

Chapter Forty-Three

THE DINNER four days ago couldn't have gone any fucking worse. I paced my room, hoping to find some respite for this god-awful knot that had been sat in the pit of my stomach for the last few days. She didn't know that we knew about what Leonard had done to her. She had no fucking idea.

After she took off after the main course, I hadn't seen her since. She'd locked herself away in her room, just like Lily had. I'd asked Grace to check in on her occasionally, if only to make sure she hadn't done something stupid. That would be something I'd never be able to forgive myself for, so I had to make sure that she was okay at all costs.

Leaving her alone to think through the events of the other night, hoping that she would still agree to help us, I'd had Grace wash the clothes she'd come here in and put them in her bedroom. I doubt she'd want to wear anything we'd put in the wardrobe, she was a creature of comfort, and if her leggings and baggy t-shirts made her feel better, then hey, who was I to stop her from wearing them. I wasn't a control freak. Damn, if I could spend my days rolling around in sweats and a t-shirt, then God knows that's exactly what I'd do.

I didn't have the time, or the energy today, to be getting myself hooked on wondering if she was okay. I had work to do. The bad kind of work. We had another one of those fuckers to deal with, one that had been on our radar for quite some time. He'd managed to slip through the net when we'd taken out another three of his ring a couple of months earlier on in the year.

He was driven here from the West Country by Hank yesterday and had been downstairs in our makeshift prison since. He'd been left to my brothers yesterday whilst I made up some bullshit excuse about having paperwork to do for my own businesses.

Since running my own companies, I didn't take part in the torturing of people as much as I used to, but sometimes they either needed my help, or I just felt like driving a knife into someone every now and then.

Dragging my sorry ass down to the kitchen, Grace had done her usual routine for when we had these kinds of *guests* and filled the cafetière ready for my pre-game beverage. It had become a joke between us all that I couldn't focus if I hadn't had my coffee, black, no sugar. I perched on one of the barstools, the aroma of coffee filling the air, and I closed my eyes for a moment inhaling deeply and focusing on the smell.

You need to get her to trust you, Tanner.

This was starting to become a constant conversation I had with myself. I didn't know what to do. I wanted to give her space, but I also wanted to kick the fucking door down and demand her to speak to me.

Staring down into the cup, the dark coffee reminded me of her eyes as it caught the lights from above, the deep shades of browns glistening in the ceramic mug. I couldn't do this today, I had to push her out of my mind, at least until I'd finished with the man being held captive downstairs.

THIS PIECE of shit was a monster.

Picking up the screwdriver with my bloodstained hands, I stepped back towards him, the weapon hanging by my side, settling it into a comfortable position. I'd stopped having to remind myself that people like him didn't deserve to walk this earth after Lily had died. Her death solidified that fact for me, making it a whole lot easier for me to do what I was about to. They deserved everything they had coming to them. They'd done some bad things, but it would catch up to them—we would catch up with them—and when we did, they would pay the ultimate price.

For someone that had been spitting obscenities about young girls in my direction for the last half an hour he'd gone pretty fucking quiet, whether he was just rude, or it had something to do with the fact I'd just taken a hatchet to his back, I wasn't quite sure. But I'd asked him nicely if he'd learnt his lesson and he'd ignored me. I'd had enough and wanted to end this so I could get back to moping around the house and eating a disgusting number of sweets whilst I watched shit TV - yes, gangster vigilantes do get some down time.

Rolling the handle of my weapon of choice in the palm of my hand, I bent my arm at the elbow, swiftly lifting it above my head before stabbing the screwdriver right into my target, pushing it further into his eye socket, until the resistance of his brain started to push back against the pressure and stopping me.

Striding away from where my last kill was still strung up by his arms, I chucked the screwdriver back onto the metal table, alongside an array of other tools we liked to use, as my brother picked up the machete and sliced through the restraints. I didn't jump when the body hit the floor with a deafening thud. I'd become used to the sound, I'd heard it so many times before, that it no longer bothered me.

Spinning round to examine my shirt under the lighting that flooded the death penalty arena, I noticed something shift out of the corner of my eye.

Riley.

Chapter Forty-Four

"Why the fuck didn't you lock the door?" I sneered at my brother, washing my hands in the sink, the crimson spinning down the plug hole as I tried to compose myself and not smash my fist into Kian's face. All he did was laugh in my face, winding me up even more than I already was.

"She didn't need to see that, what the hell was you thinking?"

"As far as I'm concerned this is our house and the bitch was snooping." He stepped in my direction, trying to threaten me, but he had nothing on me, he was shorter - weaker. Showing his psychopathic tendencies, he butted his head against mine.

Try me. Fucking try me.

"Don't call her that." Why the fuck was I standing up for her? Why was I arguing about it with Kian? Okay, so she shouldn't have been snooping, but on the other hand, he knew she was in the house, she wasn't locked in that godawful cage that she had been a few weeks ago.

"What you going to do about it, lover boy." I stayed with my head against his, like two animals about to go at each other, I held my ground, his *lover boy* comment fuelling me further. "I've seen the way you look at her, I'm not fucking stupid."

He wasn't, but maybe I was. Was it that obvious that I felt something towards her? She was beautiful, of course she was, even my prick of a brother couldn't deny that. Did I care about her though? I cared about her helping us that was for sure, but strictly for her best intentions – I think. I didn't want to see her at the hands of Leonard, and I definitely didn't want to be hearing that Leonard had managed to get his slimy hands on some other poor innocent kid.

To call me *lover boy* pissed me off though, any thoughts I had about her were strictly dick related, I kept telling myself, there was nothing else between us, other than the fact I'd like to maybe fuck her.

Who are you kidding?

Pressing my head harder against Kian's, pushing him backwards away from me, Dax entered the room, silencing whatever was about to fly out of his dumbass mouth.

"We've got to leave tomorrow morning. Make sure you're ready." Then he turned and left. Had he heard our conversation? To be honest, I didn't give a fuck if he had.

There was absolutely *nothing* between us. She was just here on secondment, helping us with business, a contractor, if you want to stick a label on it. Damn it, if they hadn't come up with this plan, then I wouldn't be butting heads with my brother over a stupid fucking girl.

Rolling my eyes, I flipped him off as I exited the room behind Dax. As much as I liked being around my brothers the majority of the time, I couldn't fucking wait for them to go away on their business trip. No idea where they were going, I couldn't remember where they'd said they were travelling to—I didn't give two shits—and I had some pretty brunette on my mind.

If I was going to speak to Riley, now was my ideal opportunity.

SECRETLY, I'd gone to visit Riley this morning and asked her to meet me in the gardens once my brothers had left for their trip. I needed to explain myself to her. I needed to make sure that she knew that I wasn't the person she thought I was. There was so much more to me than the person she'd seen drive a screwdriver into some paedophile's eye, and deep down I think she knew that.

So along with my trusty buddy, Raff—our new golden retriever puppy—I invaded her personal space, yet again, and tried to speak to her. It could have gone better, but then again, it could have gone a lot worse.

Finding her in nothing but a towel, fresh out of the shower, droplets of water still collecting on her perfect skin, I forced myself not to rip it off her body and battled with myself to stop looking at her, trying to refrain from saying something I'd probably regret.

When I asked her to see me later today, she didn't think it was a good idea—and what did I go and say—I said that it probably wasn't, but I needed her to. I could die thinking about how pathetic I must have sounded, but whatever, she said that she'd meet me there.

Whether she was telling the truth, or just that she wanted me to fuck off so she could get rid of the uninvited creep standing in her bedroom so she was able to get dressed in peace, I don't know, but I guess I'd find out soon enough.

She came down this morning after our awkward encounter for breakfast, dressed in a new pair of flat shoes I'd gone out and bought her after she nearly broke her neck the first night she was here. Sporting a semi-unbuttoned crisp white shirt, showing the perfect amount of neck, I found myself put off of the bacon that I had on my plate, the only thing on my mind was what she tasted like.

There was a lot of conversation around the table at breakfast, but as a result, she'd agreed—again—to help with the capture of Leonard. This went in everyone's favour. My brothers had people still searching his whereabouts, and they were getting close to finding him, giving them enough time to go and sort out whatever business they had to attend to and get back before he smelt out Riley.

She seemed to have the spring back in her stride, and the slight arrogance she'd show intermittently since the beginning of her stay here, had flourished into confidence. I'd done a bit of digging around, finding out things about her; what she liked to do, where she liked to go. My search results showed up next to nothing, she didn't have any specific places of interest, she'd only visited the bar that she worked in, and obviously she'd spent time at Brandon's secret apartment.

My chest tightened with jealousy as I wondered if anything had gone on between them. It was probably for the best that I didn't know - and I think I'd keep it that way. Fast forwarding through the recordings from the night Brandon had met her, until I got to the footage from the train station – the night that she looked like she was about to jump. I analysed the video, she was carrying something, a book of some sort. Inspecting further, I homed in on it, and the way she reacted when she appeared to have thought she'd lost it after Brandon had taken her down to the floor. I came to the conclusion that it must have meant something to her.

Using the key to his apartment that had been acquired from his body, I found myself driving there, hoping to find this book and whatever its contents were. Filtering through the mess that had been left there from the night before Riley came to us, I found it laying on the floor under the bed in the master bedroom. As I stood up, I flicked to the first page which read.

"Dear Diary,"

Already having invaded her personal space far too much since we met, I closed the journal and turned to the back cover. It wasn't a standard *WH Smiths* diary, it was more special than that. Punching the ISBN number into my phone and sending a text over to one of our tech guys, I asked him to see whether he could trace where the book had come from, I needed some information on where I could purchase one.

Within seconds he'd replied, he was good at his job, so it was no surprise that he'd given me all the details I needed in order to go and get her a new one. There was a small family run bookstore near where Riley's old house was that sold them, so I assumed that's where she'd purchased hers from.

So that's where I ended up. In a small book shop on the other side of town, buying a diary for some girl I barely knew, in hope that it would get her to trust me.

Or fall in love with you, dumbass.

Chapter Forty-Five

Why was I so fucking nervous. I'd been around so many girls before, and none of them had this effect on me. It was confusing, and frustrating, and I didn't know why I actually liked feeling like this when I was near her. I was an idiot, and I was on the verge of crossing the line from the safety of the shore into the choppy deep blue ocean for even giving myself the option to start feeling something towards her.

When she arrived here, she was the girl that needed saving, the girl scared of her own shadow—feisty as fuck nonetheless—but she still had this delicate nature about her, a big yellow *handle with care* label plastered across her. Now she'd become a woman, who could hold her own, and seeing her argue with my brothers over breakfast this morning just cemented what I thought I knew.

She'd wrecked everything I had planned out; I couldn't fixate my attention on anything without being reminded of her, and it was frustrating to think that it was all because of a petite brunette with eyes as wild as a forest fire and a heart stronger than anything I'd ever come across.

I'd been through shit, but I'd worked through my childhood traumas, and I never had to live first-hand the experiences that her and Lily did. I'd lost both of my parents, but then again, so had she. The difference between us both was that whilst I had my newfound family, who loved me to the core, she had no one. She had to navigate through years of seeing her father lose himself to bottles of cheap whiskey hoping that it would somehow fix the fractures that his wife's death had left across his scarred heart.

She saw him choose that over her.

She was the one who had no one but an alcoholic father who had carelessly allowed Leonard into her life.

She was the one who had been raped from the age of thirteen, with no one to turn to but a fucking diary.

She was the one who had tried to jump in front of a train.

She was the one who had found herself caught up in the crossfire, being used as a dog toy to try and get the sick bastard out of hiding.

Not me.

It was all *her*.

Something about this girl made me want to rip my heart out and serve it to her on a silver fucking platter.

I just wanted to fix her. I wanted to fix all of this.

And God knows I was about to try.

THE SUN WAS SETTING NOW, and my brothers had left the house. The sooner she came down, the better. I had so much I wanted to say to her. I didn't quite know what I wanted from this, but we'd barely spoken since the day she'd walked into the basement, and I had to let her know that I wasn't some psychopathic murderer.

My leg bounced up and down restlessly as I sat on my mother's bench, waiting for her to come and meet me – if she still planned to. Placing my hand on my knee willing it to stop, the door to the kitchen opened up and the sound of footsteps on the patio gained my attention. From the sound, I knew it wasn't Grace, her shoes had a much more clacky sound to them. I'd spent years learning what everyone's footsteps sounded like.

I remembered the sound of my father's leather brogues on the hard tile flooring, and the sound they'd make when he kicked them up onto the desk in the office after a long day of work. Hell, I even remembered the sound of my mum's high heeled sandals in the summer clicking along the cobblestones on the street from our visits to the local market when I was a kid. And how they soon became silent, as she'd mouse around the house barefooted answering the door to strange men, trying not to wake me up.

I was always awake.

In case something happened to her.

Pushing the memory far from my mind, I turned my head, my eyes instinctively meeting with hers as she gazed at me from the steps she slowly descended until we stood face to face with one another. I could feel the burn in my stomach, butterflies dancing around wildly like they would in the summer winds.

You're acting like a god damn teenager.

"Hey." She whispered softly into the air.

"Hey."

The breeze cloaked us, covering us in a blanket of warmth, whilst we stood silently under the setting sun. Strangely, there was no awkwardness between me and her, and come to think of it, there never had been, we were almost comfortable to be in the presence of each other without having to battle to make small talk.

"I brought you something." Concentrating on getting those four simple words out of my mouth without sounding like a blubbering idiot, I handed her over the parcel I'd wrapped in brown paper and tied with string. She didn't come across as the type of girl who wanted big shiny bows and fancy wrapping paper, she was a creature of simplicity, and I liked that about her. Even so, I worried that it wasn't enough.

What if I wasn't enough?

Looking down in confusion at the parcel I'd passed to her, it must have seemed like the most random thing I could have done, all things considered. Firstly, I'd been a part of her kidnapping, secondly, she thought I was using her to get to Leonard, and lastly, she'd seen me spear a screwdriver into someone's brain via their eye socket. I just hoped that once she opened it, she would see that I was way more than the monster she thought I was.

The sparkle in her eyes returned as soon as she lay her eyes on her old journal and the new one that I'd brought her at the old family-owned bookshop across town, an expression of disbelief falling across her face. That's the Riley I wanted to see more of, and if it meant I had to buy her a truck load of new journals, then so be it.

She deserved to look like that.

All of the time.

For the rest of her life.

Flinging her arms around me and nestling her face into the crook of my neck, surprised at her reaction, I held onto this moment.

I held onto her.

"Thank you."

Chapter Forty-Six

"Who hurt you, Tanner?" She asked, her voice soft like she wanted to be here with me, like she actually gave a shit about the guy who'd thrown her into the back of a van against her will.

Unlike me, she didn't have a character to uphold in this story, she could one hundred percent be herself, something I'd not been able to do, especially not in front of my brothers.

Like a tornado, she'd entered my life and flipped my world upside down, and now I found myself here trying to understand how I'd stupidly gone and fallen for her. But as we sat there, with her feet in my lap, grazing over the matters of our past like we were the oldest of friends—with no judgement and no secrets—I discovered myself opening up to the girl holding the black leatherback journal.

I told her about my mum, and her death, how I'd found her in her bedroom, lifeless. I told her about how scared I was and how I regret leaving her lying there. I spoke about how my father had found me on that bench in the park all those years ago. How he'd adopted me and given me another chance at life. Hell, I even told her about how I was basically a God at school for standing up to Durham – something which even to this day, I class as one of my proudest moments.

She laughed when I told her how everyone cheered for me when I returned back to school after my suspension, and it filled my heart with something I'd never felt. No matter how easy it was to talk to her, and how comfortable I felt whilst I was around her, I knew that I was walking into unknown territories with this girl. She made me feel like I wasn't the monster I believed she thought that I was.

"I didn't ask for him to do that to me." Defending herself, seeming not to realise that no one asks for that to happen to them.

I placed my hand on her face, cupping her chin, and forcing her to look at me with that broken look that had suddenly resurfaced.

"Don't you ever, ever, say that. It wasn't your fault. It never was. And what happens to Leonard going forward, well, that isn't your fault either."

With my thumb now skimming across her rosy cheeks, I had to stop myself from pulling her onto my lap and protecting her from those thoughts that violated her head. Her doe eyes dropped as she pressed her head into the palm of my hand.

"I think it's my daddy's fault some days, you know. He was the one who let him into our house. If he hadn't then I wouldn't be here, I wouldn't be sitting on this bench with you."

The pools of her inky night sky eyes flicked up to meet mine.

"Well, every cloud and all that."

Idiot.

She laughed under her breath and gave me a half-hearted smile.

At least she thinks your funny.

The voice in my head had a lot to say about this situation, and I could do without the intrusive abuse right now.

I pulled my hand away from her face, as she leant herself back into the bench looking up at the sky and closing her eyes. The summer breeze now moving through her hair, strands floating in the air, and I stared at her for the longest time, wondering what she was thinking about, hoping it was me.

I snapped my head away from her as she opened her eyes and hoped that I hadn't weirded her out with my inability to fucking keep mine off of her.

"Did you read my journal?" she asked, shifting her feet, and crossing them across one another, a slight guardedness in her tone. I shook my head and peered at her from the side; in my chest, I knew that she probably wouldn't believe me, but I hadn't lied to her. Not about the book anyway. Rolling her lips between her teeth, she nodded, and dropped her head back down to the leather on her lap and stilled under the starry sky for a while.

"Brandon did."

Of course, he had.

"And how did that make you feel?"

What are you, her therapist now?

"Like I wanted to die. Like I was dirty. Like nobody would want me because of what had happened."

"Never think that baby."

Baby. Really? This is what I was turning into now.

I paused, trying to find the words that would help her understand how amazing she was for overcoming everything that she'd been through. But I couldn't. With my words lodged somewhere in my throat, I placed my hand on her knee, tracing my thumb over the fabric of the black trousers that fit her frame so well. I wanted to say something. I needed to say something.

"You know, I hated you and your brothers for taking me," she sighed, "but I get it now. I get why you did it."

I twisted my body, still holding her legs in place on my lap, making sure she didn't move them from on top of me. I needed to feel her in this moment, she made me feel – safe.

"Everything should have been done differently. Kian should—" she cut me off, placing her finger delicately over my mouth, silencing my pathetic stutters.

"Shhhh. I would have done the same. I get it. You don't need to explain anything."

Her finger lingered on my lips; her eyes danced wildly with mine. With her hand on top of my own, I wrapped my fingers around it, never wanting to let go, never wanting this moment to end.

Still reclined against the back on the bench, in the safety zone, she carried on talking to me, but I had no idea what she was saying. I replied to her, but I felt as though I was on autopilot, going through the motions, with only one thing on my mind.

Rising to my feet, I placed her legs down gently onto the floor before pulling her up to meet me, I focused on her, analysing the way she returned my gaze, between the fly-away strands of hair, trying to figure out how she felt about me.

"Do you sense it? This thing between us?" I asked, lowering my head closer to her face. I wanted to kiss her, but I couldn't—not yet—I didn't want to ruin this thing between us, it was a sensitive matter and kissing her now might only make things worse.

I'd spent the last however many years making a promise to myself to never get attached to someone else, all I needed were the people who resided with me in the manor house I'd grown up in. But for the last few weeks, that notion had been tipped on its head. Her breath hitched, as I tested the waters, raising my hand to her neck, her eyes on mine, pocketing away the words I wanted to say to her.

"I know you think I'm dangerous." I managed to get out, tilting my head to the side. "I know you think that the things I do are unacceptable. My life's been far from perfect, the chaos I've been drowning in for so long gets too much some days." I paused, exploring her face for a reaction, only to find her staring back at me with the same investigative expression. "But the last few weeks have shown me that in the midst of all the anarchy, behind the walls I've built up, when I look through all the pain, there's you."

Now you're fucked, Tanner.

Closing the gap, releasing an airy breath she'd been holding in, it filled the space between us. The tips of our noses grazing against each as she rose to her toes. My heart banging wildly against my ribcage, the desire I had run through every inch of my body. Tracing a hand from her neck and down her back, the silkiness of her hair gathered between my fingers, I pulled her towards me, our bodies now pressed against each other under the stars of summer.

Tipping my head away from her slightly, allowing myself to take her in, her eyes fluttered shut as she exhaled another deep breath between her parted lips, intoxicating me, paralysing me as I was about to act on the one thing I knew may lead to our downfall. We were vulnerable and delicate. The earlier years of our lives had allowed our petals to fall and blow away in the wind, leaving thorns to grow as an armour, protecting us from others – and ourselves.

As the darkness finally climaxed, we stood together, two people who should have been sworn off each other. The son of a gangster and the daughter of a careless drunk. A tragedy waiting to be written. With my fingers entwinned with her hair and her hands pressed against my chest, we crashed our lips together, binding each other with a kiss. There was no logic, no sense to it, but here we were doing it anyway. Each touch carried with it the danger of discovery and impending doom.

My tongue traced her lips, and I felt her crumble, like the ruins of a thirteenth-century castle, beneath me, unable to withstand the intensity between us. Savouring the moment of secrecy, surrounded by the scents from the blooms of flowers that lay around us, the stars bared witness to the illicit passion we had towards each other.

"Now you can write about us."

Chapter Forty-Seven

THE FLICKERING of old black and white movies played on the TV screen in front of us in one of the more casual rooms of the house. Riley lay there with her head on my lap and a blanket shrouding her body. The tension that hung in the air around us was palpable. My gaze continued to shift between the film to her, lingering just a second more than necessary. Stroking my arm that was draped around her, I realised that emotions didn't always have to be loud or explicit, they came in many forms, softly whispering through shared moments.

The credits to the film rolled across the screen, and we stilled, her hand now motionless on my arm. I could feel my heart springing into life, and wondered if she could feel it too. I prayed that she could. I prayed that she could see the effect that she had on me.

Turning over onto her back, her head still resting on my lap, our eyes meeting whilst my heart continued to thrum in my chest. Looking down at her, she offered me a place to decompress, letting myself to get lost in nothing but the moment I spent with her.

My brothers had been away for four days now, and I found myself reliving every second I'd spent with her. Every stolen glance, every kiss we'd shared, they were all starting to amount to something more than just a need to release myself. These feelings were alien to me, I'd never let myself feel like this about someone else before, and I knew that even if I wanted to put a stop to this, it would be useless. She had a hold on me, she gave me a place to call home.

I wanted her so much that it made it hard to breathe, an asphyxiating awareness that I didn't just want her body, but her words and thoughts too. I'd had her so many times over the last few days, but I don't think it would be something I'd ever get used to. It shouldn't have been something we'd done, but we'd already crossed so many lines now, lines that we'd never be able to jump back over.

Shifting my body, positioning myself over her, her chest dipped and rose heavy and fast. She wanted this just as much as I did. Allowing my hands to glide down her body, her skin felt sensational against mine and I pulled up her oversized t-shirt and pressed my fingers into her sexy little waist. Her legs bare, I circled my fingers gently over her clit through her red French knickers, whilst my other hand remained firmly on her hip, holding her down to steady the rhythm of her bucking underneath me.

"Take it off." I ordered, pulling on the cotton t-shirt that hid her perfect body from my sight. She did as she was asked, tearing the fabric over her head and dropping it to the floor in one swift movement. She was remarkable. Everything about her drove me wild, and I didn't know how long I could keep control before I had to satisfy the need to bury myself inside of her.

Moving her hands down my back, she splayed her hands out across my tattoos when I slowly dipped two fingers into her wet pussy, she reached for my shorts, tugging them down over my hips and freeing my cock.

"You're so wet, Riley." I groaned against her thigh. "Do you know how much it turns me on when you're this wet for me?" My eyes flicked up to meet her face as I continued to drive my fingers into her, her hips now trained to the tempo of my movements. I could drown in her for the rest of time.

Tugging the lace from between her legs, I inhaled her heavenly scent, intoxicating my senses and knocking me for six, I traced my tongue around her entrance, lapping her up before teasing my way to her clit and sucking it into my mouth. With her fingers in my hair she gripped on, moaning my name as I buried my fingers deeper inside of her, pumping them wildly as I let my tongue glide up and down her folds. She was magic of the worst kind, a sweet poison that didn't have some kind of antidote to fix me, I was addicted to her, and I knew that I couldn't retreat from her now that she had me hooked.

"Tanner," she cried out, her back arching against the sofa, her eyes rolling into the back of her head. I didn't stop. There was one way this was going to end, and I wasn't going to stop until I got her there. "I think I'm going to come." She whimpered; her breathing laboured as I flicked my tongue against her most sensitive part.

"Let yourself come, *Mi Vida*. I'm hard as fuck for you. I want to feel that pussy of yours tightening around me." I pressed my mouth against her clit, sucking and licking every single bit of her. Driving my fingers back into her, she let out a melodic cry, and I swear I'd never heard anyone sing for me so perfectly. Buried between her legs with her writhing underneath me, I smiled, my lips grazing against her wet skin. I was the one who was doing this to her, I was the one who was making her feel this way, and I vowed I would never let anyone else have the chance to.

"Keep going baby, don't stop yourself." I growled gripping onto her hips tight enough to leave indents in her skin. "I want you to come for me." My thrusts now quickening inside her, plunging them deeper and deeper each time. Peering up from between her legs her hands grabbed at the blanket below her. Driving my tongue against her she moaned again and let her legs fall from my head, her body shaking as I watched over her, shuddering under the orgasm I'd given her.

Shifting my body so I hovered over her and removing my fingers, now tarnished with aftereffects of working them inside of her, I slipped them into her mouth. "See how good you taste." Without giving it a thought, she sucked the two fingers clean of her cum and my dick hardened more than I thought possible. This girl had a hold over me, fingers in her mouth or not.

The apprehension tore through me as I pressed my mouth to hers, my tongue pushing through her perfect lips to dance with hers, as our hands skimmed across each other's bare skin, shockwaves sizzling under her touch.

Moving my hand away from her mouth I placed it around her throat—she loved this—and used my other hand to rub against her clit, working her up for me to take her.

"Tanner," she whispered, "I want you to fuck me. Please." Those big brown fucking eyes of hers met mine, and I knew I was done for. Without hesitation, I kneeled in front of her, the perfection of her body enticing me more and more by the second, her chest heaving as she tried to catch her breath.

Guiding her hand down to my cock, she moved herself towards it, gliding the head around her clit, making her legs shake, before positioning it in the place I wanted it to be the most. Motioning her body onto it, causing her eyes to roll into the back of her head as I pressed into her more, giving into what she wanted. She didn't want to wait, and she let me know just that by wrapping her legs around her waist and slamming me against her, her tight pussy clenching around my shaft and I filled her sweet pussy to the hilt with every inch of me.

Using her hands and pushing against the arm of the sofa to work herself against me, I lifted my eyes to analyse her face, watching in awe as her brows furrowed and her mouth opened with each advance she made. She was a goddess, a straight up fucking divinity with fractures of light gracing her entire body, highlighting her curves more than humanly possible. She was everything.

Our bodies now grinding against each other causing the slickness of our sweat to mix together, I grabbed her wrists in one hand placing them above her before taking control and setting the pace that I knew was going to allow us to reach our climax. I stared into her eyes so deeply that I thought I might lose myself in them, there wasn't a thing in the world that mattered in this moment, all the chaos and turmoil of the last few weeks faded into nothing.

Dropping her legs from around her waist, I pulled myself out of her momentarily, staring down at her lying there on her back, out of breath, her hair wild and her eyes wilder still. I couldn't deny that I was falling more and more in love with this girl with each day that passed.

My cock throbbed as I pushed inside of her, picking up the pace and driving myself into her, harder than I thought she could take. She never failed to impress me, whether it was the way she'd dealt with all the fucking bullshit in her life, or the way that she easily took every fucking inch of me in her tight pussy, she was unbelievable. The thirst I had for this girl was all-consuming as a drove my cock further into her, my orgasm pending.

"I want you to come for me baby." I needed her to, so that I could do exactly the same. Freeing her hands, placing one on my face and the other on her clit, she circled her fingers around, before letting out another beautiful cry, the sound reverberating off of the walls caving us into the room. Her body jolted and allowed her to release herself all over me.

I'd gone from zero to one hundred, the intensity of my orgasm building deep within me, tingles shooting up my spine, tingling taking over every inch of my skin. I continued to move in her, ready to explode. Arching my neck backwards I felt as though I was levitating into the ethereal plane as I emptied myself inside of her. My arms and legs shaking so wildly that I thought I might pass out from the euphoric feeling flooding through me.

Sliding myself out of her, and flopping down on the sofa, our heavy breaths matched one another's as we lay there recovering. I didn't care if playing with her was dangerous, to me it was the greatest game on earth.

"What's on your mind?" She asked, breaking the silence, her eyes blazing into mine, as *Casablanca* started to play on the screen, the themes of love and sacrifice fit this whole situation between Riley and I a bit too well. She'd entered my life unexpectedly and flipped everything I knew a whole three-sixty. Bringing her hand up to meet my face, I knew that there was no way I could escape her, not now, not ever.

I cupped her chin, locking onto her gaze. It was

undeniable that there was something special blossoming, some kind of connection bubbling away underneath the surface, boiling point imminent. The synchronisation of deep-rooted emotions gradually setting in, and I couldn't help but fall for all of her colours whilst lost in a world of black and white.

Chapter Forty-Eight

"P-PLEASE DON'T HURT ME. *I-I just want to make sure my mummy's okay. Let me see her."*

There's so much blood, and it's coming from me.

He'd used the belt again.

My skin was torn open.

My eyes were blurry from the tears I couldn't keep at bay.

My body shook.

He raised his fist, and I hit the ground as it connected with my face.

I tried to get up, but my little body wouldn't move.

All I could do was lay there.

All I could do was wait until he killed me.

I only wanted to see my mummy.

The room closed in around me, the walls caving me in until I couldn't escape him. Bloodshed fell from the roof, raining down on top of me until I couldn't keep my head above its waves.

I'm going to drown.

I'm never going to see my mummy again.

I need to help her.
But I can't swim to the door to open it.
I'm stuck here.
I'm stuck here with him.
She left me with him.

GASPING FOR AIR trying to fill my lungs, the feeling that I was drowning still washing over me as my eyes opened, coming round from another one of my nightmares, I realised I wasn't alone.

"Shh, Tanner."

Mum?

"You're alright, I've got you, just breathe, okay?"

Riley.

"It's just a nightmare, you're fine, you're here with me." Her hand stroked through my hair, as the other warmed my face.

I nestled into her, slightly embarrassed that she'd seen me like this. I was meant to be strong; I wasn't meant to be afraid of anything, especially not a nightmare. I'd never had one of those in front of anyone but my dad. I thought I'd put those demons to bed.

Calming my breath, laying with my head against her chest, listening to the beats of her heart, I remained still until I could face her – face the shame.

"Sorry. Don't know what that was about." I sat myself round so my back was facing her, fully aware that I was being a rude fucking bastard, but I couldn't deal with her judgemental eyes on me right now. I knew exactly what that was about, and I had a feeling that she did as well.

"Why are you apologising to me?" She sounded

offended, like she wanted me to be fine about what just happened.

"Because I woke you." I said behind gritted teeth, a sense of frustration in my tone. Getting up from her side of the bed, she made her way round until she stood in front of me and climbed onto my lap. With her legs wrapped around my waist and her arms between mine and my rigid body she pulled herself closer into me. She didn't say anything. She didn't need to. Her being there was enough.

She would *always* be enough.

Placing her hands on my face, she used the power in those eyes of hers to ease my troubles. I swear the world could fall down around us, and I wouldn't even notice.

Standing up, and lifting her with me, I turned, laying her back down on the bed and settled myself next to her, her head automatically finding its place on my chest. I could feel her eyelashes fluttering against my skin as her fingers traced along the outlines of my tattoos, my body flinching as she reached one of my scars.

"Hey, you're okay."

I didn't stop her fingers from working their way across my tarnished skin, instead I let her carry on as we lay with each other, the dawn breaking outside.

"You know, I've got scars too." She said, ending the silence and taking the attention off of me. "We can be scarred together." She giggled making a joke at our misfortunes, but to me those words sounded like the most beautiful symphony ever to be written.

She was selfless, and I realised in that moment that she wasn't judging me. She never asked questions or probed me for answers, she just accepted me for all that I was and all that I had ever been. In reality, I had nothing to be scared of.

I wasn't a little kid anymore; I could protect myself and I was damn sure that I would protect her at all costs.

There's only one thing that scares me, and that's time, the lack of it and the uncontrollable hunger for more. The helplessness that comes with knowing that you may never have enough of it, and the uncertainty of being unable to tell when it will come to an end.

From the moment she'd given herself to me, I knew I had to have her. I needed her in my life, I needed her to stay here, with me, always. I would do everything in my power to make sure that she remained by my side, whatever the cost.

Chapter Forty-Nine

"Riley!" I called out up the stairs. "Are you ready yet?" My patience was wearing thin, we were meant to be going out today, and she was taking forever to get herself ready. We wasn't rushing to get anywhere, but I didn't like being away from her for too long.

Such a needy bastard.

I was like Raff, following her around everywhere like a lost little puppy, begging for her attention, something which she never denied me of. But the thing was, she was like it with me too. We'd been inseparable since my brothers had gone away on business, we had the house to ourselves, with no one here to interrupt us.

All of those stolen glances across office desks and business breakfasts had matured into touches of hands, kisses in the garden and sleeping next to each other each night. She probably doesn't know how much comfort she provides me with, and I don't think she understands that she makes me as safe as she said I make her.

I'd asked her to stay here with me. It was a dumb fucking idea, especially knowing everything that had gone on between her and Kian, but I couldn't do life without her, and for a moment, I stressed about what my brothers would say. I don't think they'd be surprised; I mean, Kian had already made diggy comments and sarcastic references about the way I look at her, and the way that I treated her, but I couldn't help but worry that I would end up as just another *bad guy* in their eyes because I'd fallen for the daughter of the enemy?

"Will you just give me a second!" She yelled back ripping me from concern. I smirked at myself knowing full well that she was most likely rolling her eyes at me. This was something she seemed to be very fucking good at.

I stood at the bottom of the stairs waiting for her eagerly, my fingers drumming against my thigh.

Fuck it.

Putting my foot on the bottom step and placing my hand on the balustrade, I shot myself up the staircase like a pinball, I couldn't wait for her anymore, she was taking too long.

"Oh no you don't." Grace's hand landed on the top of my head, as I charged towards the last step. "Leave her alone, she's getting ready, and you can't rush perfection."

"She's already perfect, Grace." This was the understatement of the year - the girl was magic.

Turning on my heels, I followed her down the stairs back into the foyer until I fell in line next to her.

"I know she is, and I'm very glad that you see that." Raising an eyebrow at me, she shot a warning look in my direction, the kind of look that says *fuck with me and you'll be in big trouble*.

Grace had grown fond of Riley, and I couldn't blame her, the girl was amazing, but I knew deep down that she saw something in Riley. She constantly made sure that she was okay, and that she had someone to talk to. She treated her as I imagined she would have treated her own daughter if she was still here, and now, she was treating me like her daughter's boyfriend.

Talk about taking sides.

I know Riley found something in Grace that she didn't get to have with her own mother, and the idea that they'd formed this relationship based on something that was forced upon them both, made it seem more genuine.

"I don't mean to pry, Tanner..."

"*But...*" I knew there was always going to be a '*but*' when a conversation that involved Riley and myself was brought up.

Rolling her eyes at me, I couldn't help but think the only two females in my life were more alike than they realised.

"*But...*" she carried on. "You need to make sure that this is something you both want, you more than her. You're both very fragile, and I think you need to realise that by falling in love with each other, the monsters from your pasts aren't going to just, well, *disappear*."

The word *love* hit me like a God damn hurricane. Did I *love* her? Was it that obvious? Were we only like this because we were searching for something to fix all of our broken pieces?

"I-I don't know if I love her."

"Who are you trying to kid?" I laughed and put my hand gently on her shoulder.

"It's hard, Grace, and I'm worried." I mumbled, trying to keep the obvious a secret.

"Worried about what? Your brothers? Or the fact that you don't want to admit to yourself that you have feelings for someone other than the people already in your life?"

Rubbing the grown-out stubble on my chin while contemplating Grace's comments, the realisation hit me square across the face.

"I know you can open up that heart of yours, there's no need to be scared. Love is a beautiful thing, you just need to take that risk for all of this worry to be worth it – and believe me, with that girl, it will be."

My life had been on auto-kamikaze mode, with no respite since I was a kid. Even when I tried to slice away at the puppet strings attached to me, there was no escape. Then coming here, I thought I had a purpose. The truth is, it turns out that the biggest plot twist of my life was up a set of stairs and three doors down the hallway, undoubtedly fussing about what to wear or how to have her hair.

"You know what you need to do, Tanner." Her voice warming the fire burning in the pit of my stomach. "Go and show her who you *really* are."

Chapter Fifty

SHE LOOKED so cute sitting in the back of the car next to me, and her hand firmly placed in mine. With her eyes wide open in awe taking in the sights as we drove through the city, it was as though she was seeing the world through a different set of lenses, seeing things she'd never set eyes on before – things that I'd seen way too much of.

Occasionally squeezing my hand with excitement and with her face almost squished against the window, I couldn't help but wonder if this is what it felt to *love* someone. Maybe Grace was right, maybe I did have it in me to love someone, to love *her*, to give her my all, my everything – the good and the bad.

Time waits for no one, and I knew that come the end of this job, if I didn't tell her how I felt, then I might lose her. For years, I'd been trying to figure everything out by myself, even when I knew I had my dad and brothers there to fight alongside me, I still felt like something was missing, and now I realised that the missing link sat next to me, filled with enthusiasm about a city we'd both lived in for our entire lives.

I didn't want her to leave once this war concluded and only have memories to hold on to. I'd seen her in so many different forms over the past few weeks, and each time I'd fallen for her just that little bit more. The adoration I had towards this girl was indescribable, how she'd made it out alive after everything she'd been through. How she held herself when faced with my brothers – and how she wasn't afraid to be herself, no matter how much the world seemed to be falling down around her. She still managed to demonstrate her integrity, even if it did come with a side of sass and dramatic eye rolls at times.

Pulling up near *Kew Gardens,* the first stop on the well-planned agenda I was proud of, the gentleman in me jumped out of the car and ran round to the other side to open the door before she could. Reaching out for her hand, I helped her out of the SUV, closing the door behind us before leaning into the front passenger side window.

"I'll call you when we're done here, then we'll be going to *Lil's.* You okay to drop us? We can get a taxi if you've got stuff you need to do?" I knew he didn't have anything else to do, but I always asked Hank, just in case he wanted some down time from helping clear up the endless mess us Lawsons left in our path.

"I'll be here when you need me, just enjoy yourself, will you Tanner. I'm hoping that girl over there might be able to tame you, and then when she does, I'm hitting retirement." Laughing, he pointed to the most beautiful girl I'd ever set sight on. The girl who looked happily lost between the sea of peonies and lavenders just inside the entrance of the gardens, the colours of the June buds shimmering against the sun's rays, highlighting her charm just that little bit more.

"Thanks Hank." Tapping the side of the car and

turning away, I made my way over to Riley who was still standing with a look of awe plastered across her face.

"You mean to tell me, you've never had instant noodles?" Putting her hand against her chest, extenuating her disbelief at my admission, almost offended that I'd never had to put those disgusting looking, cardboard tasting things in my stomach.

"Well maybe once or twice as a kid, when I was with my mum, but clearly they didn't have the same effect on my stomach as they did yours." Pretending to put my fingers down my throat and making a gagging sound, the moment was juvenile, but I had no one to act up to – I never did when I was with her. She made me want to act like an unruly teenager again, and that's exactly what I'd been doing for the last forty-five minutes as we strolled through the gardens without a care in the world, looking at the summer blossoms, each of which had been hand planted by the amazing staff here.

The place was incredible, and I was proud of myself for knowing more than eighty percent of the flower's names – something I owed to my green fingered mum. It was almost nostalgic being here amongst the gardens; I'd grown up surrounded by flowers, even when my mum relapsed, the spring bulbs that she'd planted in the window boxes continued to sprout each year, adding colours into the dark world of my childhood.

"They're amazing, you probably didn't season them enough, you don't just have to use the packet powder that comes with them. Trust me, I spent many years finding the perfect combination of flavours to accompany such a simple dish. You could use Cajun, soy sauce, sometimes I used to drop an egg into the boiling water and *boom*, you've got egg drop Ramen. When I could afford it, I'd buy some vegetables and fry them with it..."

I don't think I'd ever heard someone get so excited over all of the different ways you could cook instant noodles, yet I found myself clinging on to every word that was coming out of her mouth, even if the topic was as bland as the packeted food. Just hearing her speak warmed the gloomiest corners of my soul.

Blushing, noticing that she'd been rambling on about a whole lot of nothing for the last ten minutes, she dropped her head, slightly outraged that she'd been so eager to tell me about the past life she lived with a bellyful of Ramen.

Stopping, I pulled her into me, placing a soft kiss on her forehead. I didn't give two fucks what she was talking about, having her voice in my ear was more than enough for me.

"I've got an idea. Have you ever heard of the game twenty-one questions?" As much as I loved hearing about noodles and all the ways you could make them taste less cardboardy, I knew there was much more to the egg and Ramen girl walking along side me with her hand in mine. Looking at me confused, I explained the game to her.

"So basically, we each ask one another a question, we both answer it, until we've asked twenty-one questions, hence the name of the game. It's quite simple."

"But that means that one of us will get to ask one more question than the other, and I'm all for equality. Let's make our own game, same rules, but there's twenty-*two* questions."

"Okay, twenty-two questions." I laughed.
Damn she was endearing.

"I'll go first." She cut in. "What's your favourite colour?"

Simple.

"Grey."

"Grey?" She repeated my answer, and I could see her brain ticking away in that head of hers.

"Yep."

"Interesting."

"Okay, what's yours then, *pink*?" I jibed classing her as a typical girl, all girls favourite colour was pink, right?

"Actually, no, it's orange. So there!" She retorted, rolling her eyes, and sticking her tongue out in my direction. My skin pricked with the anticipation of what would happen later on tonight when we were at home alone together, but my god did I want to take her now.

"You know, Riley, all that eye rolling is going to get you into some serious trouble one of these days."

I loved how her cheeks altered to a deeper shade of pink when I made comments like that to her, and I wondered if I would always have that effect on her; I hope I did.

"Okay, Mr. Bigshot, what's your question?"

"What's your favourite song?"

"Easy. *Version of Me*. It's by *Sasha Alex Sloan*, her voice is incredible."

"Hmm, okay, I'll have to have a listen to it." And I would, as soon as I could, I'd listen to every damn lyric of the song, because if she was anything like me, the lyrics in the song might just open the gateway I needed into her head. I wanted to know how she felt, and what was racing through her mind, about everything, but mainly about me.

Taking away from whatever had her turning that shade of pink again, I threw my answer out there openly, hoping that she would listen to the lyrics to it. It would reveal a lot about how I felt towards her.

"Mine's *Power Over Me,* by *Dermot Kennedy.*"

"I've never heard of that, and I don't know how I'm going to listen to it." Scratching her head, and staring up at me. "I don't have anything to listen to music on back at your house."

"Oh shit, well, don't worry, that'll be sorted by the time we get home." Pulling out my phone, I tapped out a text to Hank.

> Hank, can you do me a favour? Would you mind stopping off and getting a speaker, and have it put in Riley's room please?

Within seconds my phone buzzed.

> On it! Now stop texting me!

We'd spent the last hour walking around the gardens, talking and laughing at our answers to twenty-two questions. She never fails to amaze me. She had all these dreams, of simple things that she wanted to do in her life, like swim in an ocean, and help out at homeless shelters. She wanted to write something other than diary entries, she wanted to write children's books, providing them with fantasy worlds outside of the one they lived in.

"The thing is you don't know what someone is going through. I want to give them an escape from real life. That's the point in fiction, it can take you anywhere, and sometimes, anywhere is better than where you are."

As we looked at the last few beds of flowers, the blossom

from the trees overhead fell down, covering us in whitey pinks. With the petals tangled in her hair and radiating pure enchantment, I wished I could photograph the way she looked right now and put it in my wallet to keep with me for the rest of time.

"You know what they say about people whose favourite colour is grey?" She asked, as we exited the gardens.

"Go on." Interested in hearing what she had to say, I listened in intently.

"It means that you like to be in control and don't like experiencing emotional pain, so you tend to try and shut off your emotions."

Well, ain't that the truth.

"You try to protect yourself from chaos," she giggled, and I knew automatically what she was laughing at, "and you sometimes try to protect yourself so much that you end up isolating yourself from other people."

"I feel like I'm being psychoanalysed here." I scoffed.

"No, sorry, I didn't mean to. I just find things like that interesting."

"There's something I'd quite like to know." I asked, turning to face her in between the black metal gates that lead out onto the street.

"Okay, what's that then?"

"Well," I paused, suspense hanging in the air between us. "I'd like to know what your choice in noodle seasoning says about you."

Playfully swiping out at me, I caught hold of her arm, pulling her in close to me. Our bodies flat against each other between the crowds of people leaving the gardens and kissed her so deeply, completely lost in the moment, forgetting where I was, and the reason why I was here with her.

Chapter Fifty-One

The day had gone to plan seamlessly, everything was first edition romance novel perfect. Walking out of Lil's, one of the restaurants I owned, the expression on Riley's face proved that I'd given her one of the best days of her life. I don't mean to sound big headed, but opening up Lil's was one of my greatest achievements, and I wanted to share that with her.

Like Grace had said, I needed to show Riley who I really was – that I was more than a vigilante mobster trying to rid the world of evil, one person at a time. She was too pure for me—for this world—and I needed her to see that I wasn't as bad as she thought I was, and I was worth keeping in her life.

We hadn't stopped talking, there were no awkward silences. When we were at home in our little bubble, we didn't have to worry about the outside world, we could just be us, we didn't have to put on performances, and that mirrored in the outside world – if anything, she'd shown me more of herself today than she had done since we'd taken her.

I'd started to notice more things about her, little habits she had, and the way she treated other people. She was altruistic, and kind, and respectful. She shined, and I felt as though everyone we crossed paths with could see that as well. She emanated something, that not many people in this world do – I couldn't put my finger on what it was, and maybe it was a whole lot of different things mixed together, but all it made me realise was that I needed her in my life, more than anything else I'd known. I was compelled to keep this feeling of knowing that I'm capable of feeling something, knowing that I'm capable of loving.

"Where to now?" She asked, her eyes still as wide as they were this morning, still taking in every single second of this day. The evening was setting in, and although the last of the sun still warmed my skin, I couldn't wait to get her home.

"One more place, and then we'll head back, yeah?"

Nodding in agreement, she took my hand in hers, and continued to walk along the streets, passing some other restaurants and designer shops, her eyes sparkled as we moved across the store front of a reputable high market jewellers.

"Oh my god." Her hands almost touched the speckless glass as she peered in at the jewels in the window glistening under the spotlights. The diamonds in the window didn't come close to her though.

"They're so beautiful – and *so* expensive." Choking back a laugh and looking at me surprised that someone would or could spend that amount on something they wear around their necks. She could have everything in the damn shop if she wanted.

Her eyes darted around each piece displayed out in front of her, before finally settling them on one particular item, a gold chain with an initial attached to it, a simple diamond inserted into the letter.

Get it for her.

Making the mental reminder to buy it for her as soon as I could, deciding that it would be my initial hanging around her neck, so everybody knew that she was mine.

Weather usually scared me, but the evening sun made me feel alive, especially with this girl's arm wrapped around my waist. It was unbelievable how we'd got here, and I don't think either one of us could understand how the fuck all of this had happened.

The paths were flooding with people coming out of their offices and heading into the local bars, and I wondered if they had someone at home whom they felt the same way that I did about Riley. Whether they had someone they turned to when they'd had a bad day, someone who knew all their deepest darkest secrets, someone they couldn't live without. How long had they been together, and how did they meet? Call me a hopeless romantic all you want, but I can't deny that maybe, just maybe, that's exactly what I am now. I never thought in a million years that I'd find myself being like this with someone. Not just *someone,* but the daughter of the man who had killed my father. Crazy right?

Squashing our bodies through hustle and bustle of the crowds, Riley led the way, her hand still placed firmly in mine, fitting so perfectly that it hurt.

She could hurt me. What if she does?

I paused in the middle of the street and boomeranged Riley back towards me, pressing my lips against hers for the millionth time today, exchanging the intrusive notion in my head for the touch of the only girl I'd ever been willing to give my heart to. She'd never looked so beautiful before. Her dark hair falling effortlessly down her back. Her even darker eyes bringing me a sense of hope every time she looked in my direction. Pools of deep shades of browns that I wanted to swim in forever, and given the opportunity, that's what I planned to do for the rest of my life.

"What was that for?" Her breath skimmed my lips.

"Can I not kiss you when I please?" I winked. It was definitely a wink moment. I wasn't sure who needed it more. Probably me, because I couldn't wait to get her home and in between those legs of hers I'd grown so accustomed to over the last few days, and winking was the one semi-sexy thing I could do without actually ripping her clothes off on the side of the road.

Her cheeks blushed, and she did that cute thing she does when I know I make her nervous—in a good way—without any screwdrivers and hatchets involved. Her eyes dropped to the pavement, pretending that she didn't realise that her face was flushed, and her pupils were largening.

"Come on, final stop." I grabbed hold of her hand again, and walked beside her, cloaking her in a protective shield if people got too close or looked at her for a second longer than they should under my watch.

As we stopped just off of Long Acre, I pressed myself against Riley's body, trapping her between me and the wall of the side street. Her hand met my chest, she could have felt the beating of my heart underneath it, giving away the desire I had towards her.

"Wait here." Testing my control by not taking her right

there up against the brickwork, I stepped backward, her hand dropping away from my body. I stared her up and down, tracing my tongue over my bottom lip as she leant back onto the wall, lifting one foot up and planting it onto the bricks.

Effortlessly hot.

"Don't move." Giving her a final warning glare to make sure she stayed in that very spot, I turned away and disappeared around the corner to the final destination on my mental itinerary.

Lil's Florist – another one of my business ventures.

"Hey Soph." Nodding my head towards the new school leaver I'd recently hired to help out around the shop, I was greeted by the young girl with the brunette bob, that reminded me so much of Lily's hair, dropping her phone onto the table in surprise and flashing me a suspect smile full of metal.

Busted.

"Oh, uh, sorry, hi, Tanner! I didn't know you we're due in today." No one knows when I'm due in, I never tell anyone, I just show up unannounced so I can catch my staff out blatantly on their phones instead of putting together the bouquets or funeral arrangements that had been ordered. I loved this shop, I always wondered why people were buying flowers; was it their anniversary, were they going on a first date, or were they getting them to apologise to their wives for staying out on the golf course longer than they said they would? Or simply just because they wanted to.

Giving her a side glance and an amused grin, offering a reprise that I wasn't the scary boss she probably thought I was, I meandered around the shop, brushing my hands over the countless number of flowers in the stands. The fragrances of summer buds filled the air and for a moment I was thrown back in time, where I was sitting on my mum's lap near the window of our flat, taking in the sun and floral scents of the freesias she'd bought in the local garden centre.

As I wondered around aimlessly, I could feel Sophie's eyes on me, as if she was waiting for me to ask her something. I swear females have this inbuilt radar that helps them sense the unknown, its unnerving and pretty fucking annoying if you ask me.

"Soph, if your boyfriend could pick any single flower, what would you like it to be?" My question probably came as a test to her, and I guess in a way it was, but still, I wanted the opinion from another female, as a precaution—a safety measure—just in case.

"Hmm, a *single* flower?" she pondered. "Why just a single one? Why not a bouquet?"

"Because I don't want to have to carry a bouquet home." *Lies.* It was because I'd read somewhere that giving someone a single flower—namely a rose—symbolises confidence and power. Something I definitely have, but more romantically, it indicates that they are *your* person.

I want her to always be my person.

If my brothers could see me now, standing in my own flower shop, choosing a flower for the girl we'd kidnapped, because I was so totally and inexplicably in love with her, they'd serve my balls on a platter. But in complete honesty, I didn't give a fuck. I didn't care who knew, and I didn't care what they said about it.

"I'd go with a rose, red of course, assuming this is for a girl?" Cocking her head to one side and giving me the same look I imagined Lil would have given me if she was still alive, she bounced over to the back of the shop and into the quaint preparation room.

Returning with a freshly cut red rose wrapped

delicately in a piece of cellophane, with the shop logo on, she handed it over to me giving me another one of those *girl* looks.

"So, what's she like then? How'd you meet her? What's her name?" She reminded me so much of Lily before everything went to shit, she was just as nosy and incredibly forward with wanting to know the minor details of a situation – again, another trait I think all females possess.

I grunted at her, I wasn't about to fill her in on the specifics of my love life, not when the love of my life was still waiting for my return outside. Turning on my heel and heading for the door, I turned back to Lily's doppelganger and thanked her before pushing open the door.

"You go Tanner." Soph shouted after me, and I couldn't help but smile like a goddamn fucking idiot into the streets of London. She made all the bad seem a little less depraved, slowly chipping away at the padlocks I'd fastened around my heart since I was a kid, wearing away the suit of armour I hid behind on a daily basis. This was it for me. She was everything that I never thought I'd have. Each step lighter than the last, I bounded down the street and turned down the ally, knowing she'd still be there waiting for me. She would always wait for me – and I would always wait for her.

And that's when I saw him—Leonard—right there in front of the girl I loved. His body sauntering towards her, closing the gap between them, as if he owned her, as if she was *his* property.

Seeing him there, with her, made every ounce of self-control I had in my body disperse into the city. It was like the storm that had been bubbling away on the horizon for more than a decade had resurfaced. Within a fractional second, the low rumble of thunder had twisted into a full-blown fucking explosion. Lightning bolts blinding me as the drum of thunder boomed louder than I ever imagined it would have. Flashes of anger panged through me, and I lost it. I completely fucking lost it.

Fuck this.

Shoving my phone and the rose I'd just got towards her, I told her to call Hank before charging at him. My blinkers flicked up blocking out everything around me. Before, the only thing I saw was her – now all I saw was the monster that had made my cousin kill herself and the scumbag who'd had his hands on the body of the girl I adored.

Ramming him backwards into the wall, I shoved my fist into his face, one after the other. I felt his skin splitting against my knuckles, sprays of blood flying from his mouth, and I hoped to fucking hell that he'd choke on his own teeth. He was the catalyst to my trigger, and I didn't know how much longer I'd be able to hit him without killing him—I wanted to kill him—I *would* kill him.

Eventually.

As much as I wanted to take out my gun from the inside of my jacket—yes, I carry it on me all the time, sue me—and plant a bullet directly between his eyes, I didn't want Riley to see me kill him, she'd already seen me do that once to a human, I didn't need to make it a reoccurring theme in our love story.

Just as I was about to deliver another blow, Hank interrupted and planted one into his head, knocking him to the floor.

This man had saved my ass so many times.

I watched as Leonard's body hit the concrete underneath us.

Fuck. Riley.

Sprinting over to where she was doubled over on her knees, I crouched down and took her face in my hands.

"He can't hurt you. Not now, not ever." That was a fact. He would never touch her, or anyone again.

My heart broke into a thousand fragments as I looked down at the girl in front of me, terror painted her face, as the ghost of her past lay on the floor just metres in front of us. The sorrow that had slowly started to disappear over the last few days was back, and I didn't know how to fix this for her – or if I would ever be able to fix it. All I knew was that I'd dedicate my life to trying to undo the wrongs of someone else. I'd try until my final heartbeat to piece back together the girl who was so scared and so broken, even if it destroyed me.

I craved her existence, and I knew that somehow, she would be the death of me. It's true what they say, *find what you love and let it kill you.* She was everything and now she was mine. I would burn down the world and walk through the fiery ashes beneath me to get to anyone that touched her. I would kill for her, fuck, I would die for her if it meant that she was safe.

Chapter Fifty-Two

THE MOONLIGHT FILTERED through the curtains, as I lay in my bed, a soft glow from the moon's rays cast shadows across Riley's face as she slept soundly next to me.

How did we get here?

How did we end up like this?

She was only meant to be a job, brought here for only one reason.

I wasn't meant to feel like this towards anyone, especially not her.

The memories of the last few weeks engulfed my mind, the concept of there ever being an *us* more feasible the closer we got to each other – the strange thing was, I wasn't scared anymore. I wasn't scared of giving myself to her, I would give her everything she wanted, I would make sure she was safe, and I would spend every day making sure she knew how much she was loved.

I couldn't sleep, and for the next hour and a half I tossed and turned, trying to get my mind to rest, just to give me that bit of respite that I so desperately needed. But there were bigger things going on, there was an elephant in the room, currently strung up in the basement underneath these very floorboards.

I wanted to go down there and end it, for all of us. I think I thought, that maybe if I killed Leonard, every single one of us would be able to free ourselves from the pain and angst we'd grown accustomed to over the years. I know we all felt something towards the situation, some more than others, and I wanted to draw the curtain on it, ending this act once and for all. As much as this was the one thing that I craved to do the most, I knew I couldn't. I had to wait, I had to wait for my brothers to come home from their business trip. They were a part of this too, it was their own bloodline that had been found in the bathtub, with her wrists slit and a death note placed on her side table.

It had taken me an hour or two to calm Riley down when we eventually arrived home. She looked so broken in the taxi. I didn't know what I could say to help bring back the girl who'd roamed the gardens the day before without a care in the world. She was lost again, in a world full of her own memories, memories that I wish I could erase.

We'd sat around the marble island in the kitchen with Hank and Grace, chatting about what had happened, and I think Riley was only sleeping because of the amount of wine her and Grace had sunk that evening. I didn't care what it was that was helping her, I was just glad to see her resting.

I think it gave her the confidence to ask me if she could go down and see Leonard, something I stupidly agreed to. I don't know why I let her, but she said she needed to do it more than anything. Whether it was a way for her to face her demons and to help her repair the damage he'd caused, or the fact that the two bottles of Chateau La Mission Haut-

Brion had gone to her head, I wasn't quite sure. But I agreed.

Idiot.

I know I shouldn't have, but I can't deny that seeing the confidence—fake or not—on her face when she answered back to his disgustingly degrading comments and whacked him right in the dick with a hammer, made me feel alive inside. I knew her, more than we both realised, and I realised in that moment why she wanted to come down to the basement of the house with me so much.

Setting down the small arm that was resting across my body, I pulled myself up out of bed and threw on some shorts and a white over-priced t-shirt. Rolling my eyes at the designer material, realising that all I needed was still sleeping peacefully in the bed across the room. I didn't need any of the material shit, all I needed was Riley.

We were both the same amount of messed up, and I guess I saw a bit of myself in her, someone who needed rescuing. I'd never been able to save myself, but I felt as though I could at least try to take away the demons that invaded that pretty little head of hers. Even through the continuous downpour of fucked up and agonising chaos that rained down over us, I knew that I had met her for a reason.

She makes me feel something. *Fuck*, she makes me feel everything. I don't know how, but she managed to reignite a spark that had gone out in me a long, long time ago. I don't believe in fate, I never had done, but I knew for sure that our souls didn't meet by accident.

Chapter Fifty-Three

I'D DONE everything I could this morning to pass the time, I'd cooked myself breakfast, hoovered the office and reorganised some of the books in the library. We had staff to do these jobs, but I was restless, I had to find something to pass the time until my brothers returned. I anticipated the time to when I could go and end his life. I needed Riley to wake up so I could tell her all of the ways I loved her, but she was still soundly sleeping, and she needed it, yesterday ended up in a complete shitshow, and I knew it would take time for her to recover from it.

Pacing through the hallway from the library, I made my way into the kitchen, ready for my fourth cup of coffee this morning. I didn't need it; my body was already still reeling with the adrenaline from last night and the anticipation of today. I just needed something to take my mind off of everything as best as I could.

"Hey Grace." She was standing over the coffee press, fixing a new pot ready for me, she knew me too well. Like I said before, she knew what us boys needed when we had something going down. Grabbing for the pot, she pulled my hands towards her analysing the bruising that had come out overnight.

"Oh, Tanner, love. Look at the state of your hands, let me get some ice for them." I didn't need ice, I needed to kill the cunt that was overstaying his welcome here more and more with each breath he still had the luxury of taking. Still, I knew doing these motherly things made her happy, so I let her get me some ice, place it in a tea towel and hold it against my knuckles.

She liked to do these things for us. She would do anything for anyone. The built in maternal instinct that was ripped away from her when her own child died came flooding back at every chance she got, and I wasn't going to be the one to stop her. To be honest, I appreciated it, I'd never had much of that before, and even when I did, I knew it wouldn't last long. It was one of those things I found comfort in, so I let her ice my hands, pour me a coffee and set down some pain killers on the side next to me with a glass of water.

She really was the fucking best.

"You need to stop getting yourself into all this trouble." She sighed softly as she swept the ice across my hands. "Especially now you have Riley."

"Do I though? Do I really have her?" I was so sure of everything yesterday, but then she saw him, and now I feel like we've taken ten steps backwards. I didn't know how she would feel when she woke up today. We'd put her in this position, we were the ones who had used her for our own fulfilment, and now I was questioning whether she would be able to forgive me for that.

"Tanner, love. I don't mean to get involved in yours and Riley's business, but listen to me. She adores you. Do you know how nice it's been seeing the both of you together, acting how you do when you're in one another's company?" She fussed around with the tea towel, even though there was nothing wrong with the way she'd wrapped it around my hand. "I know you Tanner, and you'll be surprised how much I've gotten to know Riley too. She thinks the world of you, and take it from me, another female who's had their fair share of upset and suffering, she wouldn't be the way she is with you if she didn't love you. It's hard to let people in when things like that have happened to you."

Grace always had a way of making sense of things, even when the creatures in my head told me everything was going tits up. She just knew what to say, and she had an impeccable talent for observing people and working out how they felt and what they were thinking, she'd read me correctly the entire time I'd been living here, not once had she been wrong about anything I'd spoken to her about. As annoying as it was, I was thankful for it, because ultimately everything she shared with me, wasn't for her benefit, but for my own.

Unwrapping my hand, the icy water now puddled on the table underneath me, like Leonard's blood soon would. Riley knew the plan, she knew that he would be killed, now not only because of Lily, but now because of her and the way her face burrowed into my chest begging me to keep her safe after coming face to face with the colossal piece of shit who had put his hands on her for all those years.

"Grace, could you go and check in on Riley please, see if she's awake yet. I'll be in the garden if she is." I needed to say everything that I wanted to before she changed her mind and ended up hating me in a way that I couldn't reverse.

"I'm on it." Throwing the floral tea towel onto the worktop by the sink, she scurried off out of the kitchen, her heels clicking on the floor, leaving the farmhouse style door to swing shut behind her.

The thunder rumbled over the house, a complete opposite to yesterday's sunshine and warmth, in a way matching the mood that was filling the house. Both the weather and I were close to breaking point, and I wondered how much longer we would be able to hold out before we both hit the apex of our emotions. Listening to the rain drumming down onto the roof I ran my fingers through my hair, tapping into every single thing I could say to Riley to get her to understand the adoration I had towards her. I wanted her to know how much I worshiped her and respected her. I needed to tell her how proud I was of everything she'd overcome. I needed to get a grip and save us.

Tell her Tanner. Tell her you love her.

Chapter Fifty-Four

SHE LOOKED SO PRETTY standing in front of me in the cream cardigan that was now soaked through, her hair sticking to her face in the heat of the summer rain. With our eyes on each other, I couldn't help but kiss her so deeply that we both knew there was no coming back from this. As our tongues danced with each other, her hands on my body told me that she wanted me too.

Our lips still touching, I found myself paralysed by this girl, everything had led to her, and I wasn't about to let her go. She said she would stay with me, but I still needed to tell her how I felt. As her eyes fluttered open, and that sexy as fuck smile crept across her face, I slowly pulled my mouth away from hers. Now was my chance.

"It's you Riley. You and only you." I had to tell her, she needed to discover how infatuated I was by her, and how my infatuation was near on an obsession. She had to understand the duty and commitment I felt towards her. It didn't lie with my brothers anymore, and I didn't even know if it lay with my father's legacy.

"It's like there's been a glitch, it's something I can't

control - even if I wanted to. *Fuck,*" I groaned, running my hands through my hair as the rain still hammered down onto us. I needed to pull myself together before I ruined my only shot at getting this girl to understand what she meant to me

A look of bewilderment flicked in her eyes. Eyes that were now filled with something that I'd never seen before, a fire that burned - for me. This was never my intention, these feelings that had grown over time were something I wouldn't have ever spoken about. They were things I wasn't ever meant to speak about, but here I was about to pour my heart out to the one person we both knew I shouldn't have fallen for.

"You know, after losing my mum, and Lily, and then my father, I'd sworn myself off of loving anyone else, because it would always, without a doubt, end tragically. I know I shouldn't want to keep you; I shouldn't be scared of what it'll do to me if you walk away, but I can't fight the war against myself any longer." I scanned her face for some sort of rejection.

"Tanner." She sighed.

Fuck. This is it.

"Call me deluded, twisted, fucked up. Call me whatever you want, but I'm happy we've had the lives we've lived, because I know that if we hadn't, we wouldn't be standing here like we are now, in this very spot getting soaked to the bone under the shitty English rain. We wouldn't be experiencing this thing between us. And I definitely wouldn't be planning a future for us in my head if I wasn't certain about how I feel." The word vomit continued. "I lost myself finding you, and I know you was out there on your own by yourself. It wasn't until you came into my life, that I became so sure of something other than the only thing I knew how to do."

Give me something Riley.
Anything.

Cupping her chin and tilting her head up, forcing her to look at me. I could die in her eyes for eternity. I was terrified but I'd never been so certain on something. I didn't know what love could mean, I didn't know how much she could mean to me, but I needed her to know that I was never going to desert her, I would never let her down.

"I-I love you, Tanner."
Well, fuck me.

And there it was again, the pinkness in her cheeks, the shortness of breath.

"I love you too, *Mi Vida*." And that was the God damn truth. Placing a delicate kiss on her forehead, I still had so much I wanted to say to her, and I didn't hesitate this time, I just opened my mouth, and let my feelings flow from my heart and out into the stormy summer skies.

"I love everything about you, every little thing you do that you think goes unnoticed, it doesn't to me. I notice it all." I whispered in her ear, our cheeks softly grazing one another's. "Like the way you chew on your little finger when you get nervous, and the way your breath hitches when I do this." I carried on, running my finger across the front of her neck and over her collarbone.

"I love the way, that with every stolen glance we've shared, every conversation we've had, each night you've fallen asleep in my arms, you've made my heart feel like it's going to explode out of my chest. But most of all, I love the way that I know you're loving me too."

"Always."
"Always, baby."

Chapter Fifty-Five

PEELING the wet t-shirt over my head I could feel her eyes on me. I liked having her eyes on me. I wanted her eyes on me for fucking ever.

"Yes, Riley?" I didn't bother to turn, because I could already feel her hands snaking their way around my torso. She was naked, her pebbled nipples brushing up against the skin of my back, making my cock twitch in my boxers. Riley knew how to get me off, she had this spark in her touch, and every time I felt it, I wanted to bury myself inside of her.

I spun around, pushing her body against the wall, knocking something off of the dresser, smashing as it hit the ground.

Did I care? Like fuck.

Her breath trapped in her throat, as I pushed her hands above her head and into the wall, stretching her naked figure out in front of me. I traced my eyes across it, taking it all in.

I loved how my hands had already explored her body, how I already felt like I knew every curve and where each scar sat on her body, but what I loved the most was that there seemed to be so much more to discover.

"I want you." She told me airily.

"I'm yours."

Grabbing her wrists and spinning her, her face now directed at the wall, I trailed my fingers along her spine, her body tensing under my touch, keeping one hand placed firmly pinning her hands on the white-washed wall. My fingers dragged down her back and over her ass, and without even being told to, she split her legs open, making way for me to enter her.

Teasing at her entrance, she was already fucking wet for me. I loved it when she was like this, she made me so fucking hard for her. Dipping a finger inside of her she moaned, arching her back and pushing herself further into me. I'd had her so many times now, but there was something about this moment that was fuelled with so much passion. Pumping my finger in and out of her, her body matched my rhythm. That was the thing about us, we were so in sync with each other, it was like we'd been together for years, we knew each other's bodies better than we knew our own, and they moulded so perfectly together.

Releasing my hands from around her wrists, I trailed them down her arms over her smooth skin before reaching her breasts, taking one in my hand and rolling her hard nipples between my fingers as she threw her head back in delight. I placed my middle finger into her mouth, and without hesitation she tasted herself off of it, making my cock grow harder.

Pushing my boxers down to release myself, I slid into her gently, tempting the both of us more with each passing second. Backing up onto my cock, her ass perfectly formed around it as she moved up and down the shaft, guiding herself with the upmost control. I couldn't take this for much longer. I was feral when it came to her. I wanted to devour her in every possible way, leaving my mark on her.

Rubbing my fingers over her clit, she bucked her hips and slid down the wall further. I knew how to work her, just like she knew how to work me. Driving into her ravenously, I fucked her like a wild animal, taking no prisoners as I felt my cock slide against her wet walls.

I needed to look at her, I wanted to see all of the ways I made her feel. Withdrawing from her, I turned her around and lifted her up onto my waist, making my way over to the bed we'd both slept in together for the past few nights. Laying her down and positioning myself on top of her, I needed to feel myself drown in her, I needed to feel her against me before we sacrificed the life we'd both known for so long.

Chapter Fifty-Six

My brother's had returned home now, and I have to admit that I think they were impressed with Riley being able to cope with everything she'd seen down there, from the first time she interrupted one of our killings to the time a couple of hours ago when my brothers discovered her in the room, watching me with him.

Riley was upstairs now; I'd told her to go and wait for me. She acted bratty – of course she did, why would she not? Reeling off shit about how she needed to be down there and see everything we did to him.

I think the fuck not.

I knew what the three of us were like when we were together doing these kinds of jobs, and even though Riley had seen me that day, driving a screwdriver into someone's eye, it wasn't planned and it wasn't into the eye of someone she knew.

I hate to admit it, but there were feelings there, she was emotionally attached to him, a damaged bond that had been seared into her throughout the years of abuse. I knew she didn't love him or anything like that, but I recognised that there might come a time when we would do something, and she would find it hard to stomach because of that underlying connection to him. It was different for us too, we never had any relation to the people we'd had in here before, we never knew the victims personally, all we knew was that we had a duty to protect and serve.

Not this time. This time, we had the cunt who had forced our own cousin into doing things she was too innocent to understand. She was too pure to be pressed into the things he made her do. Lily deserved so much more than what this world had given her, and for that, we would make him pay.

We left him hanging for hours, waiting our return, just like he'd left Riley and Lily waiting for periods of time over all of those years, never knowing when he'd be back to carry on their torment. The silence in the room was deafening, as though the ghosts of all of our pasts had caught up with us, and none of us knew what to say to one another. Everything had been prepared by Hank the night before, and he was meticulous when laying out the different tools we preferred to use.

Snatching a scalpel off our torture table, the chinking of metal on metal broke the calm as Kian moved towards Leonard without hesitation. His face expressionless. I knew him better than that, I knew that inside the anger was consuming him in the very same way it was me. Running the blade along his throat, Leonard didn't move. He stayed focused on my brother; he was a psychopath, we'd all seen a lot of shit and done a lot of shit in our time—Leonard included—to know that this wasn't going to end well for him, yet there wasn't a slither of concern about him, he'd accepted his fate, and rightly so.

"Looks like my brother beat you up pretty fucking good,

doesn't it?" Kian tormented. Out of the three of us, he was the one who loved this shit the most, I've said it before and I'll say it again, he was a sadist, born to inflict the maximum amount of pain on someone – whilst enjoying every single fucking second.

I hated to think where he'd be in life if he wasn't born into this family and into this line of work—at one of those fetish BDSM sex clubs—or in prison for murder.

"The thing is about people like you—rapists, paedophiles—you never, ever, seem to learn. You think you can swan about putting your hands on kids that can't defend themselves. You think you have the right to take their innocence, victimise them, torture them, knowing they can't do shit to stop you. Until one day, they kill themselves."

I swallowed hard as my brother's words hit home, he was talking about Lily, but I knew this whole thing with Leonard now had many more layers to it, and slowly they were starting to peel away at the surface, revealing emotions I'd stuffed away in the pocket of my black tailored suit and thrown it in the laundry in hope that it'd wash them away like it did the bloodstains.

"I think we should play a little game of hangman, for old time's sake, don't you lads?" Pointing over to me and my brother, everyone in this room knew exactly where this was going to lead, we'd all seem him pull this stunt on many men before. The look in his eyes so dark and terrifying that it was almost believable enough to think it could smother out the light of the sun.

Nodding in agreement, Kian took the blade in his hand and sliced away at the material of Leonard's shirt, revealing the piece of shit even more—burnt up arm, hairy chest and back—he was disgusting, and to think that he'd put his hands on my girl set a fire within me, the outrage burning me from the inside out.

"I think it's my turn, isn't it?" Interjecting before Kian had a chance to make his next move – one we all knew so well. Glaring over at me, the unspoken words between us transferred through the cool air of the basement. I knew he wouldn't like it, but I wanted him to let me at least start this sick game—he could end it—I didn't care, I just needed a reprieve from my thoughts right now.

Narrowing his eyes at me, he passed me the blade and stood next to Dax and gestured me to begin.

"So, we all remember how this game goes, right? I come up with a word, you guess the letter and if it's right... well, you know what happens." Of course, he did. Leonard was the one who showed us how to carve the perfect letter onto the skin of a pig in our kitchen upstairs.

Tattooists use pig skin, so they can see the needle entering the skin and learn how to control it better, it's the same way with a blade. Once you master carving something onto the skin of a pig, you'll be able to tackle the skin of a human. You want to get the angle right, the pressure right, and then you'll be set.

It was only fitting that we used this method of brutality on the teacher himself – and I was about to take great fucking pleasure in doing so.

"What letter are we going to start with then?" Throwing the question out there as if we were simply playing on a piece of paper – like I wasn't about to carve the letters into his body.

Spluttering, Leonard started to wriggle in the restraints, not that he was going to get anywhere. And even if he did manage to break out of them—which he wouldn't—Kian had already sliced through his Achilles heel, making it impossible for him to walk anywhere.

"I'm not playing." He stropped like a fucking petulant child.

"Hmm, well that's more than one letter. Want to try again?" I loved the power I felt when I had a weapon in my hand, I shouldn't but I did, especially when it came to having this scumbag in front of me – I'd been dreaming of this day for over a decade, and now I was finally living out what I only thought was a fantasy. Except now, it was real life, a real Leonard, a real blade in my hand, real blood. None of it was a dream anymore.

He said nothing, instead, his laboured breathing was the only thing filling the room, and I looked at my brothers for a hand.

"What about *N*?" Kian had this merciless grin on his face "*N* for Nonce."

"Good one." Dax knocked Kian with his elbow, and I suddenly remembered all of the fun we'd had down here. From boxing lessons, to being taught how to shoot a gun, to ridding the world of sick cunts like Leonard—well if you can call that fun, I'm sure Kian would. He had a thing for violence.

Rearranging my hand on the knife, I leant down and traced the blade across Leonard's back. There was something about the feeling of skin parting under the blade that riled me up. I wasn't always like this though. I remember the first time I stabbed someone I spent a good twenty minutes throwing my guts up in the bathroom upstairs. I had a weak stomach back then, but now, shit like this didn't bother me in the slightest, it had become like a second nature to me. I knew how to use a weapon, I'd been taught by the best, and

I'd practiced my craftmanship like a musician would practice theirs. But instead of spending hours sat at a piano, I'd spent my time down here, practicing my carving on pig skin, shooting blanks at targets, and learning how to control the inner temptation to be sick every time I saw a bit of blood.

The blade sliced through his skin faultlessly, the blood seeping out, as I began to carve the first letter of the game – N – into him. There was something spectacular about the human body, how it was more resistant to pain than we realised, how it could endure so much damage and still the heart would continue to beat through it. I guess that's what my heart had been doing since I was six years old, just beating against the pain, trying to survive as best I could, even though some days I felt as though I was being waterboarded, impossible to breathe and unable see a way out.

Crazy to think that after the years of abuse and suffering I'd been through, that I was now the one handing it out like sweets at Halloween, I guess the only difference is that these people deserved it. We would never in a million lifetimes do what the men and women we'd had down here do. We might all be fractionally fucked up, but we saw ourselves as Good Samaritans, and that's the line I'd feed myself, just to make myself feel better about taking the life of someone else.

Getting half-way through the letter, I backed up to admire my work. Leonard had really trained us well, and now it was definitely being put to good use, a saviour complex or whatever you want to call it.

"I'm not sure that's the right letter." I announced to my brothers before quickly slashing a cross through it – and my god, I had never seen anyone buck so wildly in pain. "I need a different letter, that one wasn't working for me."

Furrowing my eyebrows, I threw a look at Kian. I'd had my fun; he was up next.

"You think of one, I'm out of ideas," Kian said scratching his head. "We all know you're the cleverest out of us three." He was right, I was, but I don't think my IQ was going to end things for Leonard any less painfully.

"Well," I grinned, "what about *P* for paedophile?"

Chapter Fifty-Seven

I THOUGHT that I might had been able to convince Riley not to go down to see Leonard again, but it hadn't worked. So, now, I was standing in the basement with the girl who I'd told I loved next to me, and her abuser hanging up in front of us in an even unhealthier condition to when Riley had seen him last, and my brothers either side of where we stood. She'd already been down here twice now, and that was already two times too many.

Riley was down here because of Kian, during my time with Leonard after the game of Hangman—which by the way, Leonard didn't win—he'd gone to see her and they'd called a truce, quite a big deal for my brother dearest to apologise, but I'd take it. His way of doing this was by asking Riley if she wanted to come down to watch the finishing act. Not going to lie, I was pretty pissed that he'd asked her without my permission, but hey, I'm not the controlling type, I just want to protect her.

There was something about us all being down in this place together that bought me some kind of peace though – and everyone here deserved peace. This was the end to a story we'd all wished we could have closed the book on a long time ago, and even though each one of us had somewhat gotten on with our lives, there was always this *what if* hanging over our heads.

What if we'd seen the signs?

What if we'd tried harder with Lily?

What if we'd caught Leonard earlier?

It didn't matter about those, not now, we had him here where we wanted him.

Dax picked up one of the metal poles that leant against the wall next to him and worked his way over to Leonard, who now hung there in mid-air, and if we hadn't been so meticulous with our torture regime, you'd think he was dead already – but we knew better than that, we knew how to treat our guests to a more than satisfactory stay, without killing them straight away. We knew where to slice, we knew where to hit, we knew the points of a human body that would cause maximum pain. We knew them all like the back our hand. We were masters of our craft.

No one said a word as we waited for him to stir. Riley was shadowed away in the dark, he couldn't see her, I didn't want him to see her. I didn't want him to have the luxury of her being the last thing he saw before we killed the mother fucker.

Bearing the pole above his head, Dax throttled it into Leonard's stomach with force.

"Fuck. You." Ahh there he was. I bit down on my cheeks, using all the self-control I had mustered up inside to not bite through them, stopping myself from doing anything rash. I'd managed to keep a cool head for all this time, I didn't need to go and recklessly shoot him dead there and then, even though that's all I've wanted to do for the last twelve years.

"Nothing that these brothers have done to you will ever compare to the pain you put me through..."

What the fuck Riley?

"You can't hurt me again. I won't let you control any more of my life. You don't own me. You never did."

That's my fucking girl.

At this point in time, I was too proud to stop her, she was standing up to the one person who had caused her so much pain for all those years, so I stood there, my eyes pinned on the one person I loved most in this fucked up world, and watched on as she gave him what for. She deserved to do this – wasn't anyway she was going to touch him again, so she'd have to settle for this.

"I hope you rot in hell." Turning on her feet, she made her way back to me. I had a feeling, that in whatever life we ended up in after this one, we would always find our way back to each other.

"You cunt whore." My body tensed, like nothing I'd ever felt before.

Dax stepped forward towards Riley. "Ignore him." Almost ordering her not to turn back around and carry on towards me, her safe place. I needed her safe.

"Why don't you come over here and suck it one last time for old time's sake?"

Is he fucking serious.

My blood curdled in my veins as I breathed deeply, focusing every ounce of self-control I had not to go over to him and rip his heart out of his fucking chest. He deserved everything that had happened to him. I would never let anyone speak to Riley like that again, and if they did, then they'd pay the ultimate price.

I watched on as Riley froze and I examined her face, trying to figure out if she was breaking inside like she had done so many times before, and I wondered if I'd have to piece her back together, and how I could.

But then it happened.

It happened so quickly.

Without a fucking warning.

Grabbing the gun from the table and cocking it with ease, just like I'd taught her, she paced back towards him.

"Why don't you suck on this? Cunt."

And she pulled the trigger.

She pulled the fucking trigger.

Chapter Fifty-Eight

THE LAST FIVE days had been weird to say the least. Leonard was gone, and my girl was the one who had killed him. Not that my brothers or I cared all that much. It was quite cinematic how he ended his life; at the hands of the last girl he'd put his dirty hands on.

It was a big fucking bravo moment if you ask me, and if this was a Broadway show, I'd have been there in the front row with a standing ovation and yelling for an encore. Unfortunately, that's not how Riley had seen it. She'd spent near on a week asking us if she was going to get caught, whether she would end up in prison. As much as we reassured her that there was no way that would happen, I knew that every time I looked at her, that she was battling a war against herself, one that was happy Leonard was gone, but also one that made her a murderer.

The skies were clearer today, for the first time since we cut Leonard's lifeless body down from the rafters of the basement. I didn't know what today would bring for us, I didn't know if today was going to be a better day than the one before, but all I knew, was that I needed the girl who was lying in bed next to me with her doe eyes looking into mine, forever.

"Tanner, I wish we could leave this place."

Say no more.

"I know baby." And that was something I did know because that's exactly what I wanted too.

Reaching for my t-shirt and trousers, I threw them on, telling her to stay here—knowing that she probably wouldn't, she was too nosey for her own goddamn good—but I had one final bit of business that I needed to take care of. Racing down the stairs and hallways to our office, I barged in, I didn't have time to mess around.

"I want out, Dax." Spinning on his chair, my brother peered over his newspaper at me without the look of surprise I thought he might have had on his face. Instead, he had that same warmth I remembered him having when he used to let me stay with him when I first got here, the same depth that had once given me the strength to stand up to people, the same understanding he'd shown me when we stood in that hospital room when dad had died.

He knew.

"I know."

Pushing my hands through my hair, I knew that this could put a divide between us and everything I'd known since I was ten, but Riley meant more to me than any of this.

"Dax, I'm sorry. I can't do all of this anymore..." waving my hands at the corruption that fell around the room; the safes with the guns and money in, the artwork that hung over secret entrances. "Not when I have someone that I want to start a life with... Someone I want to start a family with."

That's all I wanted to do now. I didn't want to be a part

of this anymore. It had never been in my nature to do the things I had, and I guess that's why I'd never been a part of anything other than what went on down in the basement. I'd told myself that I was doing something good in the world by eliminating the bad from it, and I don't regret it, I'd never killed someone that didn't deserve it, but I was done with it.

"I want to be with her. I want to be with her without having to worry about anything happening to us." I felt as though I was putting forward my case in the Supreme Courts, fighting for my freedom before someone locked me up and threw away the key.

"You know what will happen, if you go."

Of course, I fucking did, no protection, no money from the criminal side of the business. I didn't care. I didn't care if I had to start over. I just had to get out.

"I can't let you do this. You have to stay." Riley's voice suddenly came from behind me.

"Riley, shut the fuck up." I probably shouldn't have spoken to her like that, but she didn't get it. If we stayed here, we could never have the life that she wanted, the life that she deserved.

"Dax, I would like to go with them." Hank's voice fell next to me, and I faltered. What the fuck was going on? "I hope you understand the demons this place holds for me." And again, for the millionth time since Riley walked into my life, my heart shattered inside of me. I'd never tried to comprehend how Hank had felt being surrounded with the constant reminders of what happened to Lily and my father. It must have been just as hard for him as it had been for us.

There was a silence, like the calm after a storm, when the sun comes out and everything seems clearer. I think, that if I'd never met Riley, I would have just carried out my days living this life, just like my father had, until maybe one day a drunk would mow me down, and I'd die laying in a hospital bed on my own, because I sure as hell wouldn't have had kids to surround me as I took my final breaths.

All I knew was that I wanted to follow her. I wanted to walk along the same path that she did. Everything I am now, and everything that I ever will be is because of her.

I want to love her in every way possible – always.

One Year Later

Chapter Fifty-Nine

Riley

I LOVED it here in St. Albans. The charming city made me feel a little more *human*. No drugs, no murders, no guns—okay, well, Tanner and Hank still had their guns—just as a safety precaution, and to be honest, I was fine with that.

I had a nice life now, a life that I never thought in a million years I'd be able to live. I had my own little café, where I served homemade cakes. Turns out I'm actually a dab hand when it comes to flour, eggs, and sugar, regardless of my instant noodle upbringing. I'd started writing the children's book that I'd always wanted to write on my new MacBook, courtesy of Tanner. I'd managed to find someone to do the illustrations for me once the manuscript was finished, and I couldn't wait to be able to hold it in my hands once it was. It would have been my biggest achievement by far.

When we moved here a year ago, I found it hard to adjust to normal life—we both did—which was understandable. All we had ever known were lives of darkness and chaos, and suddenly, we'd come face to face with the sunlight and calm of this cute city. It was completely juxtaposed to London. St. Albans was quiet and beautiful, it was everything I'd ever dreamed of, but it was a big change.

We wanted a normal life, so that's what we went and achieved. We threw away the fancy clothes for jeans and trainers, got rid of the violence and guns—bar the aforementioned—for rolling pins and pinafores, and left the manor house for a quaint Tudor period four bed detached property.

Hank and Grace decided to come with us, and the relationship with Tanner's brothers hadn't been damaged as much as I thought it might have been, especially when I believed they thought I'd stolen him away from them. They'd been to visit a couple times and were no doubt scouting out potential business around here they could invest in. Both of them had taken a back seat with all things drugs related, selling off contacts and suppliers to other people interested in that field of work.

Kian was still as hot headed as ever, but I thought it was best not to ask if they were still involved in the one thing that had kept the three of them bound together for so long. Dax seemed calmer, he didn't have that seriousness about him constantly, and we'd heard from Kian that he'd been dating someone, although Dax was more than happy enough to squash that notion pretty quick.

There wasn't any trouble around here like there was in London, the worst I'd seen was an argument between two men in their fifties who had been leaving a bar, one attempted a punch, but lost his footing and ended up falling into one of the ponds outside. Funny as opposed to frightening.

It was peaceful here, boring, but peaceful. Did I miss London? A little, but I wasn't too sure why, I guess the only thing I could put it down to was the fact that I'd spent my entire life there, the good and the bad parts. London would always be deep-rooted in me, no matter how much I wanted to let parts of it go.

All I knew was that I didn't miss it enough to want to move back there. It could have been voted the best place to live in *Country Life* but there were too many negative reminders to warrant living there again.

I know Tanner missed it, maybe not all the time, but there were definitely occasions when I believed he wished he could go back. I think he missed the excitement that his old life provided him, the tracking down, the capturing and the exile of *bad* people.

I caught him and Hank in the garden the other day, playing 007 with their guns, throwing themselves around on the floor like kids, as if they were evading shots from a make-believe villain, and pretending to shoot back at them. They even high fived each other when this invisible person got hit by a fake bullet for Christ's sake.

I didn't question him on it, I didn't want to start a conversation that might lead him to tell me how much he missed London and that he wanted to go back there. I didn't want to give him a reason to start resenting me because I didn't want that life he'd known since he was ten years old.

At the end of the day, I already blamed myself enough for taking him away from everything he knew, even if he reassured me every day that this is what he wanted as well. It was better if I just kept quiet when I caught him doing odd shit like that, even if some days it ate me up from the inside out.

Today was a good day though. I was working—like a normal person—and serving the customers whom I'd grown to know and love fondly. Everyone here was so friendly, they were so welcoming when we moved here, it was like they rolled the red carpet out to everyone who set foot upon the cobbled streets. Everyone seemed to adore Tanner, why wouldn't they? And to say he was a hit with the older ladies was an understatement. We'd been here for four full seasons now, and I'd seen him help the elderly residents planting bulbs and pulling weeds in the spring, mowing their lawns and watering plants in the summer, sweeping leaves from their driveways in the autumn and running them to the shops when it snowed in the winter. He was elite, and I was lucky he was mine.

Looking over at my boyfriend who was sitting with Josie and Pam, two of the ladies who ran the pub quiz we'd go to every Friday night, I wondered if he was really happy here.

Was I enough for him?

I had something to tell him, and I hoped that if I wasn't enough on my own, then maybe the baby growing inside my belly would be.

THE END.

Acknowledgments

Mum, you've been my number one fan since I said that I was going to start writing again. Thank you – for everything. For raising me, looking out for me, and being my best friend. Thank you for everything you have done for me, and for being my number one supporter. Thank you for the endless hours you've listened to me going on and on about ideas for this book, and for being there with me through this journey. I love you more than I could ever say! P.S. Thanks for reading the smut and not being cringed out haha!

When I came up with the idea of the Lawson's I was sat around my friends table, with a glass of wine and four hyper as fuck kids, doing God knows what in the background. I didn't know if the concept would work, or whether anyone would even bother to read it, but she told me something, she told me to go for it. If I hadn't, the Lawson's would still be an idea scrawled down on a crumpled-up piece of paper. She's celebrated my victories with me, listened to me moan about deleting half the manuscript because I hated it and everything else in between. But most of all she's been my best friend through this journey. Ash, thank you for being you, thank you for being the sun and thank you for being *my person*.

Frankie, my little boy, my greatest achievement – DO NOT READ THESE BOOKS!!!! Keep shining and being you, never change. I love you all the stars in the sky baby.

Lea and Leanne, my dream team, without you girls, this book would still be a very badly edited document on my laptop. Thank you for making my work come to life again.

H – still and will forever be my MVP.

And lastly, my readers. I can't thank you all enough, for making this whole journey what it is, for your love and support, for actually reading my books, it's still a fucking wow moment every time I see that someone's read something I've written. I will be eternally grateful. Love you guys!

Printed in Great Britain
by Amazon